Through A Glass, Darkly

Also in the Crime Classics series:

Through A Glass, Darkly

Dr Basil Willing Investigates

HELEN McCLOY

SIRIUS

ABOUT THE AUTHOR

US mystery writer Helen McCloy (1904–1994) was the first woman to serve as president of Mystery Writers of America. In addition to her Basil Willing series of thirteen novels, she wrote a further sixteen mysteries. She is widely regarded as one of the best detective writers to have come out of the United States. Elegantly written and subtly plotted, her stories are satisfying as well as enjoyable.

SIRIUS

This edition published in 2017 by Sirius Publishing, a division of Arcturus Publishing Limited,
26/27 Bickels Yard, 151–153 Bermondsey Street,
London SE1 3HA

Design and layout copyright © Arcturus Holdings Limited
Text copyright © Helen McCloy, 1949

Cover artwork by Steve Beaumont, coloured by Adam Beaumont
Typesetting by Couper Street Type Co.

ISBN: 978-1-78828-276-5
AD002458UK

Printed in Canada

For Chloe

*'Little green shoot that came
up in the Spring'*

CHAPTER ONE

You have the face that suits a woman
For her soul's screen,
The sort of beauty that's called human
In Hell, Faustine.

Mrs Lightfoot was standing by the bay window. 'Sit down, Miss Crayle. I'm afraid I have bad news.'

Faustina's mouth held its usual mild expression, but a look of wariness flashed into her eyes. Only for a moment. Then the eyelids dropped. But that moment was disconcerting – as if a tramp had looked suddenly from the upper windows of a house apparently empty and secure against invasion.

'Yes, Mrs Lightfoot?' Faustina's voice was low-pitched, clear – the cultivated speech expected of all teachers at Brereton. She was tall for her sex and slender to the point of fragility, with delicate wrists and ankles, narrow hands and feet. Everything about her suggested candour and gentleness – the long, oval face, sallow and earnest; the blurred, blue eyes, studious, a little near-sighted; the unadorned hair, a thistledown halo of pale tan that stirred softly with each movement of her head. She seemed quite composed now as she crossed the study to an armchair.

Mrs Lightfoot's composure matched Faustina's. Long ago she had learned to suppress the outward signs of embarrassment. At the moment her plump face was stolid with something of the look of Queen Victoria about the petulant thrust of the lower lip and the light, round eyes protruding between white lashes. In dress she affected the Quaker colour – the traditional 'drab' that dressmakers called 'taupe' in the thirties and 'eel-grey' in the forties. She wore it in rough tweed or rich velvet, heavy silk or filmy voile according to season and occasion, combining it every evening with her mother's good pearls and old lace. Even her winter coat was moleskin – the one fur with that same blend of dove-grey and plum-brown. This consistent preference for such a demure colour gave her an air of restraint that never failed to impress the parents of her pupils.

Faustina went on: 'I'm not expecting bad news.' A deprecating smile touched her lips. 'I have no immediate family, you know.'

'It's nothing of that sort,' Mrs Lightfoot answered. 'To put it bluntly, Miss Crayle, I must ask you to leave Brereton. With six months' pay, of course. Your contract provides for that. But you will leave at once. Tomorrow, at the latest.'

Faustina's bloodless lips parted. 'In mid-term? Mrs Lightfoot, that's – unheard of!'

'I'm sorry. But you will have to go.'

'Why?'

'I cannot tell you.' Mrs Lightfoot sat down at her desk – rosewood, made over from a Colonial spinet. Beside the mauve blotter were copper ornaments and a bowl of ox-blood porcelain filled with dark, sweet, English violets.

'And I thought everything was going so beautifully!' Faustina's voice caught and broke. 'Is it something I've done?'

'It's nothing for which you're directly responsible.' Mrs Lightfoot lifted her eyes again – colourless eyes bright as glass. Like glass, they seemed to shine by reflection, as if there were no beam of living light within. 'Shall we say that you do not quite blend with the essential spirit of Brereton?'

'I'm afraid I must ask you to be more specific,' ventured Faustina. 'There must be something definite or you wouldn't ask me to leave in mid-term. Has it something to do with my character? Or my capability as a teacher?'

'Neither has been questioned. It's simply that – well, you do not fit into the Brereton pattern. You know how certain colours clash? A tomato-red with a wine-red? It's like that, Miss Crayle. You don't belong here. That must not discourage you. In another sort of school, you may yet prove useful and happy. But this is not the place for you.'

'How can you tell when I've only been here five weeks?'

'Emotional conflicts develop rapidly in the hothouse atmosphere of a girls' school.' Opposition always lent a sharper edge to Mrs Lightfoot's voice and this was unexpected opposition, from one who had always seemed timid and submissive. 'The thing is so subtle, I can hardly put it into words. But I must ask you to leave – for the good of the school.'

Faustina was on her feet, racked and shaken with the futile anger of the powerless. 'Do you realize how this will affect my whole future? People will think that I've done something horrible! That I'm a kleptomaniac or a Lesbian!'

'Really, Miss Crayle. Those are subjects we do not discuss at Brereton.'

'They will be discussed at Brereton – if you ask a teacher to leave in the middle of the fall term without telling her why! Only a few days ago you said my classroom was "most satisfactory".

Those were your very words. And now . . . Someone must be telling lies about me. Who is it? What did she say? I have a right to know if it's going to cost me my job!'

Something came into Mrs Lightfoot's eyes that might have been compassion. 'I am indeed sorry for you, Miss Crayle, but the one thing I cannot give you is an explanation. I'm afraid I haven't thought about this thing from your point of view – until now . . . You see, Brereton means a great deal to me. When I took the school over from Mrs Brereton, after her death, it was dying, too. I breathed life into it. Now our girls come from every state in the Union, even from Europe since the war. We are not just another silly finishing school. We have a tradition of scholarship. It has been said that cultivation is what you remember when you have forgotten your education. Brereton graduates remember more than girls from other schools. Two Brereton girls who meet as strangers can usually recognize each other by the Brereton way of thinking and speaking. Since my husband's death, this school has taken his place in my life. I am not ordinarily a ruthless person but when I am faced with the possibility of your ruining Brereton, I can be completely ruthless.'

'Ruining Brereton?' repeated Faustina, wanly. 'How could I possibly ruin Brereton?'

'Let us say, by the atmosphere you create.'

'I don't know what you mean.'

Mrs Lightfoot's glance strayed to the open window. Ivy grew outside, freckling the broad sill with patches of leafy shadow. Beyond, a late sun washed the faded grass of autumn with thin, clear light. The afternoon of the day and the afternoon of the year seemed to meet in mutual farewell to warmth and brightness.

Mrs Lightfoot drew a deep breath. 'Miss Crayle, are you quite sure you can't – guess?'

There was a moment's pause. Then Faustina rallied. 'Of course I'm sure. Won't you please tell me?'

'I did not intend to tell you as much as I have. I shall say nothing more.'

Faustina recognized the note of finality. She went on in a slow, defeated voice, like an old woman. 'I don't suppose I can get another teaching job, so late in the school year. But if I should get a post next year – can I refer a prospective employer to you? Would you be willing to tell the principal of some other school that I'm a competent art teacher? That it really wasn't my fault I left Brereton so abruptly?'

Mrs Lightfoot's gaze became cold and steady, the gaze of a surgeon or an executioner. 'I'm sorry, but I cannot possibly recommend you as a teacher to anyone else.'

Everything that was childish in Faustina came to the surface. Her pale tan lashes blinked away tears. Her vulnerable mouth trembled. But she made no further protest.

'Tomorrow is Tuesday,' said Mrs Lightfoot briskly. 'You have only one class in the morning. That should give you time to pack. In the afternoon, I believe you are meeting the Greek Play Committee at four o'clock. If you leave immediately afterward you may catch the six twenty-five to New York. At that hour, your departure will attract little attention. The girls will be dressing for dinner. Next morning, in Assembly, I shall simply announce that you have gone. And that circumstances make it impossible for you to return – greatly to my regret. There should be hardly any talk. That will be best for the school and for you.'

'I understand.' Half blinded by tears, Faustina stumbled toward the door.

Outside, in the wide hall, a shaft of sunlight slanted down from a stair window. Two little girls of fourteen were coming down the stairs – Meg Vining and Beth Chase. The masculine severity of the Brereton uniform merely heightened Meg's feminine prettiness – pink-and-white skin, silver-gilt curls, eyes misty bright as star sapphires. But the same uniform brought out all that was plain in Beth – cropped, mouse-brown hair; sharp, white face; a comically capricious spattering of freckles.

At sight of Faustina, two little faces became bland as milk, while two light voices fluted in chorus: 'Good afternoon, Miss Crayle!'

Faustina nodded mutely, as if she couldn't trust her voice. Two pairs of eyes slid sideways, following her progress up the stair to the landing. Eyes wide, but not innocent. Rather, curious and suspicious.

Faustina hurried. She reached the top, panting. There she paused to listen. Up the stairwell came a tiny giggle, treble as the hysteria of imps or mice.

Faustina moved away from the sound, almost running along the upper hall. A door on her right opened. A maid, in cap and apron, came out and turned to look through a window at the end of the hall. Her sandy hair caught the last light of the sun with a gleam like tarnished brass.

Faustina managed to compose quivering lips. 'Arlene, I'd like to speak to you.'

Arlene jerked violently and swung round, startled and hostile. 'Not now, miss! I have my work to do!'

'Oh . . . Very well. Later.'

As Faustina passed, Arlene shrank back, flattening herself against the wall.

The two little girls had looked after Faustina slyly, with mixed feelings. But this lumpy face was stamped with one master emotion – terror.

CHAPTER TWO

What adders came to shed their coats,
What coiled, obscene,
Small serpents with soft, stretching throats
Caressed Faustine?

Faustina entered the room Arlene had just left. There was a white fur rug on the caramel floor. White curtains framed the windows. The chest of drawers was painted daffodil yellow. On the white mantelpiece stood brass candlesticks with crystal pendants and candles of aromatic green wax made from bayberries. Wing chair and window seat were covered with cream chintz sprigged with violet flowers and green leaves. The colours were gay as a spring morning, but – the bed was unmade, the scrapbasket unemptied, the ashtray choked with ashes and cigarette-butts.

Faustina closed the door and crossed the room to a window seat where a book lay open. She turned the pages in frantic haste. A tap fell on the door. She closed the book and thrust it down behind a cushion, straightening the cushion so there was no sign that it had been disturbed.

'Come in!'

The girl on the threshold looked as if she had stepped from an illuminated page of Kufic script, where Persian ladies, dead two thousand years, can still be seen riding mares as dark-eyed, white-skinned, fleet, and slender as themselves. She could have worn their rose-and-gold brocade with grace. But the American climate and the twentieth century had put her into a trim grey-flannel skirt and a pine-green sweater.

'Faustina, those Greek costumes . . .' She stopped. 'What's wrong?'

'Please come in and sit down,' said Faustina. 'There's something I want to ask you.'

The other girl obeyed silently, choosing the window seat instead of the armchair.

'Cigarette?'

'Thanks.'

Slowly, precisely, Faustina put the cigarette-box back on the table. 'Gisela, what is the matter with me?'

Gisela answered cautiously. 'What do you mean?'

'You know perfectly well what I mean!' Faustina spoke in a dry, cracked voice. 'You must have heard gossip about me. What are they saying?'

Long black lashes are as convenient as a fan for screening the eyes. When Gisela lifted hers again her gaze was non-committal. One hand made a little gesture toward the cushion beside her, trailing cigarette-smoke.

'Sit down and be comfortable, Faustina. You don't really suppose I have a chance to hear gossip, do you? I'm still a foreigner and I came here as a refugee. No one ever trusts foreigners – especially refugees. Too many were maladjusted and ungrateful. I have no intimate friends here. The school tolerates me because my German is grammatical and my Viennese accent is more pleasing to Americans than the speech of Berliners. But my name, Gisela von Hohenems, has unpleasant connotations so soon after the war.

So . . .' she shrugged, 'I spend very little time over teacups and cocktail glasses.'

'You're evading my question.' Faustina sat down without relaxing. 'Let me put it more directly: have you heard any gossip about me?'

The pretty line of Gisela's mouth was distorted by that expression our friends call 'character' and our enemies, 'stubbornness'. She answered curtly: 'No.'

Faustina sighed. 'I wish you had!'

'Why? You want people to gossip about you?'

'No. But since they are gossiping, I wish they had gossiped with you. For you are the only person I can ask about it. The only person who might tell me what is being said and who is saying it. The only real friend I've made here.' She flushed with sudden shyness. 'I may call you my friend?'

'Of course. I am your friend and I hope you're mine. But I'm still at sea about this. What makes you think there is gossip about you?'

Carefully Faustina crushed her cigarette in the ashtray. 'I've been – fired. Just like that.'

Gisela was taken aback. 'But – why?'

'I don't know. Mrs Lightfoot wouldn't explain. Unless you call a lot of woolly platitudes about my not fitting into the Brereton pattern an explanation. I'm leaving tomorrow.' Faustina choked on the last word.

Gisela leaned forward to touch her hand. That was a mistake. Faustina's features twisted. Tears sprang into her eyes as if a cruel, invisible hand were squeezing them out of her eyeballs. 'That's not the worst.'

'What is the worst?'

'Something is going on all around me.' Words tumbled from Faustina's mouth as if she could not contain them a moment longer. 'I've felt it for some time. But I don't know what it is. There are all sorts of indications. Little things.'

'Such as?'

'Look at this room!' Faustina made a bitter gesture. 'The maids don't do things for me as they do for you and all the other teachers. My bed is never turned down for the night. Half the time it isn't even made. There's never any ice water in my thermos carafe and my room is never dusted. I have to empty my scrapbasket and ashtray myself. Once the windows were left wide open all day so the room was freezing cold when I went to bed.'

'Why didn't you complain to Mrs Lightfoot? Or the housekeeper?'

'I thought of it, but – I was new here this term and the job meant a lot to me. And then I didn't want to get Arlene into trouble. She's the one who's supposed to do my room and I've always felt sorry for her. She's such an awkward, tongue-tied girl. At last I spoke to her myself. It was like talking to a deaf person.'

'She didn't hear you?'

'She heard all right, but she didn't listen. There was something obstinate and resistant under her blank surface that I couldn't reach.' Faustina lighted another cigarette, too self-absorbed to offer the box to Gisela. 'Arlene wasn't impudent or sullen, just – withdrawn. She mumbled something about not realizing my room had been neglected. She promised to look after it in future and then – she didn't. This afternoon she avoided me almost as if she were afraid of me. But, of course, that's silly. Who would be afraid of a bookworm like me?'

'Is Arlene's attitude all you have to go on?'

'Oh, no! Everyone avoids me.'

'I don't.'

'Gisela, honestly, you're the only exception. If I ask any of the other teachers to tea in the village or to cocktails in New York, they refuse. Not just once or twice, but always. Not just two or three teachers, but all of them – except you. And they refuse in a queer self-conscious way, as if there was something wrong with me. A week ago, in New York, I passed Alice Aitchison on Fifth Avenue, opposite the Library. I started to smile, but she – she looked the other way, pretending she didn't see me. Yet I know she did. It was quite obvious, really. Then, there are the girls in my classes.'

'Are they insubordinate?'

'No. It's not that. They do everything I tell them. They even ask me intelligent questions about their lessons. But . . .'

'But what?'

'Gisela, they watch me.'

Gisela laughed. 'I wish my pupils would watch me – especially when I'm demonstrating something on the blackboard.'

'It's not just when I'm demonstrating something,' explained Faustina. 'They watch me all the time. In and out of the classroom, their eyes are always following me. There's something . . . unnatural about it.'

'Especially in the classroom!'

'Don't laugh,' protested Faustina. 'This is serious. They're always watching and listening. And yet . . . sometimes I have the queerest feeling that – that I'm not the one they're watching.'

'I don't understand.'

'I can't explain it very well because I don't understand it myself, but . . .' Faustina's voice sank. 'They seem to watch and listen as if they were waiting for something to happen. Something I don't know about.'

'You mean as if they expected you to faint or go into hysterics?'

'Perhaps. I don't know. Something like that. Only I never have fainted or gone into hysterics all my life . . . And there are other things. For one, they're too polite to me. For another, when I meet any of them in the driveway or the hall, there's a look in their eyes that's curious and knowing. As if they knew more about me than I know about myself. And there's a tendency to giggle as soon as my back is turned. Not the happy giggling of normal schoolgirls, but a nervy giggling that sounds as if it could pass into crying or screaming very easily.'

'What was Mrs Lightfoot's attitude when she asked you to leave?'

'Cold at first and then – she seemed almost sorry for me.'

Gisela smiled wryly. 'That's the queerest thing you've said yet. Mrs Lightfoot seems hard and self-centred.'

'There must be some reason for what she did,' went on Faustina. 'It's costing the school six months' unearned salary to dismiss me in mid-term. And the loss of a fairly competent art teacher, who will be hard to replace so late in the school year. But she was very firm about it. I can't even use her as a reference if I apply for another teaching position.'

'You've a right to some explanation,' mused Gisela. 'Why not get a lawyer to talk to her?'

'I'd hate that. It would get around. Other schools wouldn't like the idea of engaging a teacher who calls in her lawyer at the first sign of trouble.'

'She really has you in a cleft stick, hasn't she?' Gisela sighed and leaned against the cushion at her back.

It was harder than a cushion should be. She shifted her position and the cushion toppled to one side. Turning to straighten it, she saw the corner of a book behind the cushion – an old book, calf-bound and gilt-tooled, with a crumbling edge.

'Oh, I'm so sorry.' Faustina snatched the book and cradled it in both arms, tight against her flat chest. Gisela could not see the title.

'You must have been so uncomfortable!' Faustina apologized.

'Not at all. I didn't know the book was there till just now.' Gisela rose, all in one lithe movement, with the boneless grace of a kitten. A shade of coolness crept into her voice. 'Sorry I can't be more help.' She moved toward the door, then paused and looked back. 'I almost forgot what I came for. I was going to ask if you'd have the costume designs for the Greek play finished by tomorrow. Now I suppose you won't bother with them.'

Faustina was still standing by the window seat, clutching the book tightly. 'They are finished already and Mrs Lightfoot wants me to submit them to the committee before I go.'

'All right. We're meeting in my room, you know. At four.'

Gisela crossed the hall to her own room. After she had closed the door, she stood still for a moment, frowning. Then she went to her secretary and unlatched the glass door of its bookcase. The books were neatly arranged on three shelves without a gap, but those on the lower shelf seemed to fit more loosely than usual. Her searching glance came to rest on a set of several volumes, calf-bound, gilt-tooled, with a crumbling edge. Volume One was missing.

Still frowning, she sat down at the desk. Four sheets of white notepaper were spread out on the dropleaf – three already covered with handwriting; the fourth, a blank. She drew it toward her and began to write:

P. S. Did you ever happen to read the Memoirs of Goethe*? I have the French edition translated by Madame Carlowitz and Faustina Crayle has borrowed the first volume without the formality of asking permission. I only discovered it by accident, just now, when she tried to hide the book from me. Why she wanted it, I have no idea. I wouldn't attach any importance to it, if it were not for the way that everyone here treats poor Faustina, as I've already written you. Some word must have reached Mrs Lightfoot for Faustina herself tells me she has been asked to leave.*

There is something sinister about the whole affair and, to tell you the shameless truth, I'm beginning to be a little bit frightened myself. More than ever, I wish you were in New York. I know that you would find some reasonable explanation for the whole thing. But you're not here and so . . . I can't go down the upper hall after ten, when the blue night-lamp is the only light, without looking back over my shoulder and expecting to see . . . I don't quite know what, but something distinctly peculiar and unpleasant.

Gisela laid down her pen and read what she had written with a look of indecision. Without giving herself time to change her mind, she folded the four sheets, stuffed them into an envelope, sealed, and stamped it. She took up her pen once more and wrote on the envelope:

Dr Basil Willing,
18-A Park Avenue,
   New York, New York   *Please Forward*

She slipped a fur coat over her sweater and skirt and hurried downstairs with the letter.

Outdoors, the chill wind of a November twilight nipped her cheeks and disarranged her hair. Clouds, grey but still faintly luminous, raced raggedly before the gale. She walked through a rustle of fallen leaves, covering the half-mile to the gate in a few minutes.

Another girl was standing beside the RFD box that faced the highway.

'Hello, Alice,' said Gisela. 'Has the evening mail been collected?'

'No. Here he comes now.'

Alice Aitchison looked about nineteen, but a certain hardiness and freedom marked her as a young teacher rather than an old pupil. She was a ripe, autumnal beauty with brilliant hazel eyes, honey-coloured skin, and full lips painted a fruity red. Her suit was the same nut-brown as her hair. A vivid scarf of burnt orange filled the open neck of her jacket. She smiled as an old Ford car rattled to a stop and a man in mackinaw and shoe-packs clambered down.

'Two more letters just in the nick of time!' Alice took Gisela's letter and gave it to the postman with her own.

'Okay.' He dropped them into his sack. 'You womenfolks here sure have a big correspondence. Boy friends, I suppose,' he added, with an amiable wink.

The Ford was wheezing on its way as they turned back toward the house.

'Your – ah – boy friend a doctor?' demanded Alice.

Gisela looked at her in surprise. Alice was rather coarse in speech and manner when none of the elder teachers were about, but she was supposed to be well brought up – not the sort of girl who would read superscriptions on other people's letters.

'Yes. A psychiatrist. Why do you ask?'

'Thought I'd seen that name somewhere before – Basil Willing.'

Gisela was amused. 'He's fairly well known. And now that's settled, there's something I want to ask you.'

'Fire away.'

'You've been here longer than I have,' began Gisela. 'And . . .'

'Don't remind me!' Alice interrupted sourly. 'Five solid years of this manless world! Just like living in a convent or a women's prison!'

'Five? I thought this was your first year at Brereton too.'

'Before that I was four years at Maidstone. Not as a teacher – just a pupil. I lived for the day when I'd be graduated. What a wild life I was going to have! You'd be surprised if I told you the plans I made then.' Her eyes looked beyond Gisela, sullen and brooding. 'It was just three weeks before my graduation that my father shot himself.'

'Oh.' Gisela was at a loss for words. 'I'm sorry. I didn't know.'

'Only a year ago, but no one remembers it now.' Alice looked at her defiantly. 'Just another Wall Street speculator who bet on the wrong horse and couldn't take it. I was left with nothing. I heard Mrs Lightfoot was looking for a dramatic coach. So I asked Miss Maidstone to recommend me. I thought Brereton might be an improvement on Maidstone. It isn't. I'm sick unto death of the whole thing. I want a job in New York where I can live like a human being.'

'Was Maidstone just like this?' asked Gisela.

'Same principle, different application. Maidstone is supposed to be more modern and hygienic. The girls drank milk, hiked, and slept in haystacks. The simple life at a luxury price. Visitors allowed only on Sunday afternoons and even then under supervision. My poor father thought it would be good for me, but it only made me more determined than ever to get out into the real world.'

'Whether you like Brereton or not, you're more at home here than I am,' went on Gisela. 'Your work brings you into a closer relationship with the girls, and you're nearer their own age. They might talk to you when they wouldn't talk to me.'

Alice threw a guarded glance at Gisela. 'About what?'

'Faustina Crayle.'

'I don't know what you're talking about.'

'I believe you do,' retorted Gisela. 'I've seen the way you look at her sometimes – with unfriendly curiosity, as if you thought there was something odd about her.'

'Nuts,' said Alice, rudely. 'Faustina Crayle is just a fool. Nothing odd about that. It's only too common. She's weak and shy and colourless and desperately anxious to please. No sense of humour. No gift for making friends. An old maid in the making. A natural-born victim. Miss Faustina Milquetoast. The sort of person who is always taking vitamin pills without the slightest effect. You've noticed the little bottle of riboflavin *et al.* beside her plate at table, haven't you? There's nothing you can do with people like that.

Their character is their fate. She was born to be the butt of every humorist and every bully and – there's quite a bit of the bully in Old Heavyhoof.'

'Old Heavyhoof?' repeated Gisela, uncertain of the new American idiom.

Alice grinned. 'The girls' name for Mrs Lightfoot.'

'Then,' resumed Gisela thoughtfully, 'if Faustina were to lose her job, it might be simply because she hadn't enough character to make a good teacher?'

'Could be.' Alice was eyeing Gisela speculatively. 'Has she lost her job?'

'That's not my business or yours.' Hastily Gisela changed the subject. 'Do you suppose . . . would it be possible for me to recover that letter I just mailed? If I telephoned the postmaster in the village and explained that I wanted it back?'

Alice let loose a peal of harsh laughter. 'My dear girl, your letter is now in the custody of Uncle Sam's mail. You'd probably have to hack your way through a jungle of red tape and fill out fifty forms in quintuplet. Even then, I doubt if you'd get it back. Why do you want it? Pretty hot stuff?'

'Of course not.' Gisela was annoyed.

'What then?'

'I wrote a postscript on impulse. Now I wish I hadn't. It's probably what you call in America a wild goose's nest.'

'You mean a mare chase?'

They had reached the front door. Alice turned the knob and pushed. 'That's funny. It's locked.'

Gisela pressed the bell. They stood shivering in the wind while daylight faded and darkness drew in around them.

'Oh, hell!' Alice exclaimed. 'Let's go in the back way. It's always open.'

Gisela agreed, though she suspected Mrs Lightfoot did not care for such informalities.

They plodded along the path that circled the house, their hatless heads bent against the wind, their gloveless hands thrust into their pockets. The drawing-room windows were dark, but as they rounded a corner of the house, light shone cheerfully through the dusk from a row of kitchen windows. Alice opened the back door. Gisela followed her inside.

In this old country house the kitchen was larger than the drawing-room in the average New York apartment. A kitchen planned in the days when cooks were plentiful and wages low, so no one counted the steps it took to prepare a meal. The modern equipment – white stove, stainless-steel sink, and electric refrigerator – looked out of place in that great room with its row of curtained windows and its floor of oak planks, scrubbed and waxed every day.

The cook was at the sink, peeling and washing brussels sprouts. From the oven came an aroma of roasting chestnuts to mix with them. The centre table was piled high with an armful of autumn leaves and flowers – chrysanthemums, asters, oak leaves, and sumac. Faustina was arranging them in a large vase of Steuben glass – a regular duty of junior mistresses at Brereton. She was dressed for outdoors in a blue covert topcoat and a brown felt hat.

Alice paused. 'Were you outside just now?'

'Yes.' Faustina looked at her with vague surprise.

The door of the back stairs opened. Arlene stepped down into the kitchen. She was carrying a small tea tray in one hand.

'I've been in the cutting garden for the last half-hour.' Faustina answered with more heat than such a casual question warranted. 'Why do you ask?'

'Oh . . . I just wondered.' One dark brow was lifted and a corner of the ripe mouth quirked – a nice blend of disdain and disbelief. 'Thought I saw your face at an upstairs window just now while we were coming up the drive.'

There was a crash of shattered glass and china. Arlene's tray had fallen to the floor.

The cook cried out sharply: 'Can't you ever mind what you're doing, Arlene? Two more teacups gone! When I was a girl, we were trained to be careful of good china, but you're all thumbs these days. What's the matter? In love?'

Arlene stood still, looking at Faustina with frightened eyes.

'You get a brush and dustpan and clean up that mess,' went on the cook. 'I shall tell Mrs Lightfoot to take the price of the china out of your wages.'

'I wish you'd let me pay for it!' Faustina spoke impulsively to the cook. 'After all, it was I who startled her.'

Alice had watched the whole scene with avid interest. Now she broke in: 'Don't be silly, Faustina! You didn't do a thing.' Alice turned to Gisela. 'Did she?'

'No.' Gisela spoke with reluctance. 'Nothing that I saw.'

This answer seemed to disturb Alice. But she said nothing more until she and Gisela were alone, crossing the dining-room to the hall. 'I suppose you realize that five girls have been taken away from Brereton just since school opened?'

'No. I knew that three girls had left, but I didn't realize it was as many as five.'

'And two of the maids departed rather suddenly.' Alice turned to look at Gisela. Light from the hall doorway spotlighted her expression – bright eyes, mocking red lips twisted in a derisive smile.

'Let me tell you something, Gisela von Hohenems. If you wrote your psychiatrist friend anything about Faustina Crayle – you'll be sorry!'

CHAPTER THREE

Wine and rank poison, milk and blood
Being mixed therein . . .

Gisela's feeling of uneasiness persisted all next day, quite out of proportion to the few facts she knew about Faustina. But some echo of a similar situation seemed to lie just below the threshold of Gisela's conscious memory. Emotions associated with those other, forgotten facts were reaching the level of consciousness in the form of a haunting sense of evil. She was like the shell-shocked man who cowers at the sound of an explosion without knowing why he does so. Once again she realized that emotions circulate more freely than facts or ideas through the various planes of consciousness.

She had little hope of an immediate reply from Basil Willing. His last letter had come from Japan. For all she knew he might still be overseas with the Navy. She had written him largely because she had no one else to confide in.

She did not see Faustina again until the meeting of the Greek Play Committee. Alice was the first to arrive, a cigarette dangling from one corner of her mouth.

'What's all this about Faustina being fired?' she asked with lazy insolence as she curled up on the window seat.

'That's all I know about it,' returned Gisela. 'The bare fact that she's leaving.'

'Why?' insisted Alice.

'I don't know.'

Neither Gisela nor Alice heard the door open, but now Faustina stood on the threshold, a portfolio of sketches under one arm. 'I did knock,' she said timidly. 'I suppose you didn't hear me. I could hear you talking so I came in.'

Alice looked up at her sardonically. 'Don't worry so much about your manners, Faustina. I'm sure you did everything quite correctly.'

Faustina's hand was trembling as she unfastened the portfolio. 'I just didn't want you to think I was eavesdropping.'

'And why should we think a thing like that?' demanded Alice.

Faustina spread her sketches on the table. Then she looked at Alice deliberately. 'I don't know why, Alice, but you always seem to suspect me of something like that.'

Alice laughed. 'Hoity-toity! Temper, temper!'

Faustina winced. 'How can you speak to me that way?'

Gisela picked up a sketch in watercolour of a woman wearing ancient Greek dress. 'Is this the costume for Medea?'

'Yes.' Faustina seemed glad Gisela had changed the subject. 'I spent an entire morning doing research for that one costume. The peplum is over her head because that's the way it was worn by a woman in times of grief or mourning. And Medea is in a state of grief from the beginning of the play. The folds should be arranged as gracefully as possible. A peplum worn clumsily was a sign of provincialism.'

'Then I think Medea should wear her peplum clumsily,' said Alice promptly. 'Wasn't she a barbarian?'

'A barbarian who had lived for many years in Greece,' amended Gisela. 'And a princess as well.'

'The corners should be loaded with little weights,' went on Faustina. 'Like the lead dress-weights our grandmothers wore in the hems of their long skirts.'

'What's the other thing on her head?' asked Alice. 'Looks like a bushel basket.'

'It's a mitry,' exclaimed Faustina. 'The bushel-shaped crown of Ceres. Many Greek women wore them.'

'Medea wouldn't pattern herself after a glorified domestic-science teacher like Ceres. Medea was a feminist and a witch.'

'I'm not so sure,' put in Gisela. 'Primitive women are proud of their association with bread-making. The very word "lady" means "loafgiver".'

'Would you rather she wore a tiara?' offered Faustina. 'Like Hera and Aphrodite?'

'I'd much rather,' insisted Alice.

'I can change the mitry to a tiara easily,' agreed Faustina. 'What about her footgear? Do you like the flower-embroidered sandals?'

'I wish I had a pair just like them,' said Gisela quickly. 'They're charming.'

But Alice was looking at the sandals with distaste. 'Too conventional. Why not laced shoes lined with cat's fur, the muzzle and claws used for decoration? Greek women did wear that sort of shoe, and think what fun we'd have killing and skinning a cat! Or two cats. One for each shoe.'

'Why not skin the cat alive?' remarked Gisela. 'You'd enjoy that, Alice, wouldn't you?'

Alice was unabashed. 'You think I'm pretty savage, don't you? The truth is I'm merely bored with the life I live here. I'd do anything for a little excitement.'

'What about Jason and Creon?' Faustina held out two more sketches.

'I like them,' said Gisela. 'Jason has all the handsome stupidity of the professional soldier and you've made Creon president of the local Rotary Club, Greek style.'

Abruptly, Alice let out a hoot of raucous laughter.

'Faustina, you are priceless! Don't you realize you've made Medea a harlot?'

'What do you mean?' Faustina was embarrassed.

'That tunic and vest. They're hyacinth blue – the colour reserved for prostitutes.'

'Oh.' Faustina appealed to Gisela. 'Is that true?'

'I'm afraid it is,' admitted Gisela. 'Though I hadn't thought of it.'

'Of course it's true,' said Alice, imperiously. 'Haven't you ever read about Ceramic, the red-light district of Athens? If a man named Theseus wanted a particular woman named Melitta he would write on the wall with a piece of charcoal: "Theseus loves Melitta." If she accepted him, she'd write underneath: "Melitta loves Theseus," and wait for him there with a twig of myrtle between her teeth.'

'But wasn't that only in Athens?' objected Faustina. 'This play takes place in Corinth.'

'Then you'll have to put in another morning's research finding out what the harlots wore in Corinth!' Alice seemed to enjoy the prospect of more work for Faustina. 'Or perhaps you know already? I imagine you know quite a lot about the traditions of prostitutes. Ever hear of Rosa Diamond?'

Faustina's face flushed a morbid crimson. 'No. And anyway

I can't do another sketch because I'm leaving this afternoon. For good.'

'Lucky you!'

'I'm not lucky. I don't want to go.'

'Then why are you going?'

Again Gisela intervened. 'There's no reason why you should do another sketch for Medea's costume. It's easy enough to change the colour when we choose the material. What about pale yellow? That would go just as well with the flowered sandals as hyacinth.'

'As you please,' said Alice, indifferently. 'What's this thing?' She picked up another sketch. 'Looks like a Hoboken imitation of a Paisley shawl.'

Faustina turned stricken eyes to Gisela. 'That's the poisoned robe Medea gives to Jason's bride. It's called "multicoloured" several times in the text. I copied the design from a photograph of a Greek vase about the same period as Euripides. Only, in place of violets in the original pattern, I used a foxglove leaf because foxglove is a poisonous plant.'

'Would Medea telegraph her punch like that?' objected Alice. 'If anyone sent me a robe embroidered with foxglove leaves, I'd be suspicious. So would any reader of detective stories.'

'But Creon's daughter was not a reader of detective stories,' said Gisela. 'It's a nice touch of symbolism. Just what a believer in magic, like Medea, would do.'

'What about the colours?' went on Alice. 'They look Persian to me.'

'Persians and Greeks did influence each other,' pleaded Faustina. 'That's one of the interesting things I found out doing research. You know when you're looking up any one thing, you always find so many other things that have nothing to do with the thing you're looking for. Did you know that the Sybarites gave their dinner invitations one year in advance, so they would have plenty of time to plan their food and dress with the maximum of luxury? And that the Greeks played tennis? It was a Spartan game and they played it nude.'

'Congratulations, Faustina! You've done a very thorough job of research.' Alice was really enjoying herself now. 'The next time I go down to the tennis court, I shall go completely nude. And when Mrs Lightfoot objects, I'll say: "Oh, it was Faustina Crayle's idea. She said that the Greeks always played nude and that I really ought to try it."'

'But I didn't say you ought to try it!' Faustina was almost in tears. 'Please don't do that, Alice!'

'I most certainly shall.' Alice's eyes were dancing with malice.

'You most certainly shall not,' said Gisela. 'Don't let her fool you so easily, Faustina.'

'Oh, I see – it's a joke.' Faustina was pale again and quite serious. 'If that's all, I'll leave these other sketches with you and just take the one of Medea, so I can alter the mitry this afternoon before I go.'

When the door had closed on Faustina, there was a brief silence. Then Alice cried out defiantly: 'Don't look at me that way! I can't stand people like that. They need to be stirred up.'

'Do they? You were brutal, Alice. It was so – unnecessary just as she's leaving.'

'You're soft.' Alice crushed out the last of many cigarettes and rose. 'Someone should teach Faustina to hit back.'

'By bludgeoning her almost insensible? That's what you did psychologically.'

Alice paused in the doorway. Her ripe, brown beauty had never looked more sultry. She started to speak. Then she muttered: 'Oh, hell!' and went out without another word.

When Gisela's last class for the day was over, she went out for a walk around the grounds, hoping that physical exercise would purge her mind of ghosts from the subconscious.

It was one of those deceptive fall days when the clear sunlight looks warm and feels cold. A pathway wandering through the woods brought her to the creek that bounded Brereton land. She took another path on the way back and came out of the woods at a lawn which sloped up from the creek to the house. She paused as she saw someone sketching at an easel in the centre of the open space.

It was Faustina.

She was wearing her blue covert coat again, but this time her head was bare. The level rays of the afternoon sun gilded the pale halo of hair, giving her whole face an unaccustomed radiance. Her back to the house, she was sketching the view from the lawn – a row of willows along the creek and a sparsely wooded hill on the other side of the water where each leaf stood motionless in the windless day, clear-cut against a brilliant blue sky. There was a paintbox at her feet, a small palette in her left hand. She handled her brush with quick, deft strokes, so intent on what she was doing that she did not seem aware of Gisela.

Moving softly on rubber-soled brogues, Gisela took a few steps nearer to get a glimpse of the sketch without disturbing Faustina. Then something happened – something so inexplicable that Gisela stopped short.

Faustina was still intent on her sketch. The hand that held

the brush still moved with skill and precision only – it had lost its swiftness. Quite suddenly every movement she made was languid and weighted as the movements of figures in a slow-motion picture.

In that still, sunny afternoon, time itself seemed to be slowing down, like a clock that needs winding. The universe was not exploding as some modern physicists claim – it was expiring quietly out of sheer exhaustion . . . Then a breeze sprang up and stirred the branches overhead. They moved at normal tempo. Only Faustina Crayle was moving more and more drowsily, as if the brush would drop from her listless fingers in another moment. There was something utterly horrible about that sudden fading of her life impulse. It was much like a machine running down because power is being drawn off for some other purpose . . .

How long she stood there, Gisela never knew. She was roused by a cry that made her forget everything else. It came from one of the open windows behind Faustina.

Gisela ran to the nearest window. She found herself in the library. It was empty and still, except for one curtain that shuddered in the breeze. It was dim, for dark shades were half drawn against the golden lances of the late sun. The hall door was closed. Another door stood ajar. Through this opening came a shrill voice shaken with sobs:

'Oh, Beth! Don't! Please! Oh, what shall I do?'

Gisela hurried through the doorway, into a smaller room furnished with writing-desks. Here the curtains were blowing wildly, for the hall door stood open, opposite the open windows.

Meg Vining was crouching on the floor. Her face, usually so pink and pretty, looked almost ugly now – blanched and tense.

Beside her, on the floor, lay Beth Chase, limp, unconscious. Her freckles were no longer comical. They stood out brown as old ink-stains against a face that had gone ghastly pale.

Gisela knelt swiftly, chafing the little girl's cold hands, feeling for a pulse so faint that it eluded her first touch.

'Shock.' Her steady voice quieted Meg's wailing. 'Tell the housekeeper to bring blankets and hot-water bottles.'

'What happened?'

The quavering voice was Faustina's. She was standing outside an open french window, her eyes wide with amazement. She still held a wet paintbrush in one hand. Behind her was the view she had been painting – the lawn sloping down to the creek and the hill rising to meet the sky. She took a step forward to cross the threshold.

Meg Vining screamed. 'Don't! Don't come near me!'

'Margaret! Control yourself.' Gisela was surprised at the sharpness of her own voice. 'Faustina, get the housekeeper, please. Tell her to bring blankets and hot-water bottles. Beth Chase has fainted. Hurry.'

'Of course.' Faustina went through the door into the hall.

Gisela took off her own jacket and wrapped it around Beth, cradling the girl in her arms.

'What happened?' she asked Meg, her eyes still on Beth's ghastly face.

'I . . . don't know.'

Gisela turned to look at Meg. 'What do you mean? Something must have happened.'

Wild-rose colour flooded Meg's cheeks. Her lower lip set obstinately. 'I don't know what made Beth faint, Miss von

Hohenems. It must have been something she saw. Or perhaps she's ill. She just cried out and toppled over.'

Gisela heard rapid footfalls coming down the hall. She would have only a moment more alone with Meg. She tried to put that moment to good use.

'This is serious, Margaret. I want the truth. What is it?'

Meg's eyes looked bright and cold as blue diamonds.

'But I've told you the truth, Miss von Hohenems.' Her voice was brittle.

'And I think you haven't.' Before Gisela could go on, Mrs Lightfoot burst into the room, followed by Faustina and the housekeeper, carrying blankets.

It was Mrs Lightfoot who carried Beth upstairs. Gisela had never seen this side of the woman's character before – a balked maternal tenderness finding outlet in the care of other people's children. She was not thinking of herself or her school as she made Beth comfortable in her own bed. There was genuine relief in her sigh as colour came back slowly to the pale, pinched cheeks and a dew of perspiration darkened the light brown hair at the temples.

At last Beth lifted sandy lashes and looked about the strange room.

'What . . . where . . . ?'

'Keep still and try to rest,' said Mrs Lightfoot, gently. 'The housekeeper will sit by your bed and get you anything you want.' She rose and looked at the other faces. 'Thank you, Miss von Hohenems, for acting so promptly. Margaret, I want you to come down to my study with me.'

'Yes, Mrs Lightfoot.' Once again Meg's face was pink and smooth as she followed Mrs Lightfoot out of the room.

Going down the hall to her own room Gisela heard hasty footsteps. Faustina drew abreast of her, panting a little. 'Why didn't Mrs Lightfoot say a word to me? This is my last day. A taxi is coming for me in an hour. Couldn't she have been a little more civil?'

'Have you any idea what made Beth faint?' countered Gisela.

'No, I haven't. Have you?'

'I had my back to the house.'

Faustina paused as they came to the door of her room. 'I was painting there for about twenty minutes. Then I heard a child scream. I was so startled, it took me a moment or so to collect myself. You know how it is when you are absorbed in something like painting or writing. I turned around and I couldn't see anyone. But the windows were open, so the scream must have come from one of them. I ran to the one that was nearest me – the writing-room window.'

'Did you see me running toward the library?' asked Gisela.

'No, I didn't. You must have reacted more quickly than I did. By the time I reached the writing-room, you were there, kneeling on the floor beside Beth.'

'I went through the library to the writing-room,' said Gisela. 'But you came straight to the writing-room from the lawn. Yet it took you longer.'

'I was so startled,' Faustina's eyes begged forgiveness. 'And I'm never as quick as you are.'

'You stood at a window directly opposite the door into the hall. That door was open. Did you see anyone in the hall?'

'No . . . no . . .' Faustina's brow puckered and she spoke uncertainly. 'I can't say I saw anyone . . .'

'Did you see anything at all?' demanded Gisela, impatiently.

'Now you mention it, I did have an impression of something moving out there in the hall. But the light was dim – with those Venetian blinds half drawn against the sun. And I wasn't really paying attention to anything in the hall. I was looking at you and Beth in the writing-room.'

'I saw you painting as I came up the path from the creek,' went on Gisela. 'Even then you were moving slowly – more slowly than usual. Did you feel ill?'

'Not ill. Just sleepy. I could hardly keep my eyes open. It was that awful scream that woke me. You know how fear can wake you suddenly? Even when you're really asleep, a nightmare will wake you.'

'So you were frightened?' asked Gisela.

'Yes. Weren't you?'

'I suppose I was. But not enough to slow down my reactions. Do you feel all right now?'

'Oh, yes,' Faustina sighed. 'I'm just a little – tired.' She smiled wanly.

'Let me help you pack,' suggested Gisela.

'Would you? That's really kind. But there isn't much to do. I did most of it this morning. And I have so few things.'

When the last of two rather shabby suitcases was strapped and locked, Faustina took a book from her bedside table – an old book, calf-bound, gilt-tooled, with crumbling edges.

'This is yours,' she said with a trace of embarrassment. 'Volume One of your Goethe *Memoirs*. I took the liberty of borrowing it one day when you were out. Something I wanted to look up.'

'Thanks.' As Gisela took it she glanced at the flyleaf. In old ink, faded to a light brown, someone had written in a spidery, Italianate hand: *Amalie de Boissy Neuwelcke, 1858*. Once again something seemed to stir on the edge of her mind just beyond the reach of memory . . . 'Come over to my room and have a cup of tea before you go,' she suggested. 'You still have a few minutes until your taxi is due.'

Daylight was fading as they entered Gisela's room. She switched on a lamp shaded with amber silk. She made tea in an old-fashioned silver set with a spirit lamp to heat the water, and served it with lemon.

'To your future!' Gisela raised her cup gallantly as if it were a glass of wine. 'May your next job be a better one!'

But there was little gallantry in Faustina. She set down her cup after the first sip. 'I have no future,' she said blankly.

'Nonsense. Drink your tea while it's hot. It will make you feel better.'

Obediently, Faustina drank. She was always acquiescent. Or was a better word for her 'suggestible'?

'Thank you.' She put down her empty cup. 'And now I'm off. I can't keep that taxi waiting. I don't want to miss my train to New York.'

'I'll go down to the door with you,' said Gisela. 'Don't forget to write me as soon as you have a permanent address.'

They went out into the hall. Faustina made a forlorn little figure, leaving the school for ever, on a chilly autumn night, in a thin spring coat of blue covert, with only one person of all those at Brereton willing to go down to the door and wish her Godspeed.

She was walking a few steps ahead of Gisela when they turned a corner and came to the head of the stairs. Light from a pair of sconces in the upper hall shone down as far as the first landing. Below, the stairway was in deep shadow, for there was no light in the lower hall yet.

On that first landing, in the full glow of the light, stood Mrs Lightfoot, perfectly immobile. One hand rested on the balustrade, as she looked down the stairs into the dark hall below. Her frosted flaxen hair was newly coiffed in smooth coils and she was dressed for the evening in cameo colours – an outdoor wrap of taupe velvet, falling in heavy folds to her ankles, just revealing a chiffon skirt and the toe of a satin slipper all the same colour. There were touches of white at her throat – ermine and gardenias, a glimpse of pearls. The velvet sleeves were elbow length. Below them she wore long, wrinkled gloves of immaculate white. Her eyes were still focused intently on the shadows in the lower hall as her voice rang out crisply:

'Miss Crayle!'

'Yes, Mrs Lightfoot?' Faustina spoke from the head of the stairs.

Mrs Lightfoot started violently and turned to look up at Faustina. There was a moment of breathless silence, broken by Faustina:

'You called me?'

Mrs Lightfoot spoke in a voice that lacked her usual aplomb. 'How long have you been standing there?'

'Only a moment.' Faustina smiled hesitantly. 'I was in such a hurry that I had an impulse to slip past you on the stairs. But, of course, I didn't. That would have been awfully rude.'

'Yes, it would.' Mrs Lightfoot compressed her lips. 'Since you're in such a hurry, don't let me detain you, Miss Crayle. Good night.'

She went on down the stairs, a graceful figure in flowing velvet, carrying her back straight and her head high, as the women of her generation were taught to do.

Faustina and Gisela followed at a discreet distance.

Mrs Lightfoot had reached the last step, when Arlene, in black dress and white apron, came out of the drawing-room into the lower hall and switched on the lamp there. The sudden blaze of light showed the hall empty, looking just as usual. There was no clue to suggest what had drawn Mrs Lightfoot's gaze below when she stood on the landing.

'You're late, Arlene.' Mrs Lightfoot spoke irritably. 'You should turn on this lamp before it gets dark on the stairs. Someone might fall.'

'Yes, ma'am,' Arlene answered sullenly.

Mrs Lightfoot smoothed one of her gloves with elaborate casualness: 'Did you see anyone just now? In the hall? Or in the dining-room as you came through from the pantry?'

'No, ma'am. I didn't see a soul.' Something like malice touched Arlene's lips. 'Did you?'

'Of course not!' But Mrs Lightfoot's voice had lost authority.

Stillness was shattered by the peal of a telephone bell. Mrs Lightfoot started as if that sudden clamour were almost more than her nerves could bear. It came to Gisela, with the shock of revelation, that someone or something had frightened Mrs Lightfoot almost as much as Beth Chase . . .

Arlene went to an extension in the closet under the stair. 'The Brereton School . . . What name please? . . . One moment . . . For you, Miss von Hohenems. Long distance, person to person, from a Dr Basil Willing.'

CHAPTER FOUR

A shadow of laughter like a sigh,
Dead sorrow's skin . . .

He had known she would wear black. She was a European and a Viennese of Chanel's generation – how could she ever feel really dressed in anything but black? It was dull crêpe this time, cleverly fitted at the waist, flowing more freely about slender feet in stockings sheer as black shadows and the flimsiest of high-heeled sandals. No sleeves or straps broke the firm line of her white shoulders. There were no jewels at her throat or in her hair. But something about the way she carried her head suggested a flash of jewels – the ghost of forebears who had worn coronets. Her hair was cut a little shorter now and brushed back above her ears. Under its sleek, dark waves, her face bloomed pale and delicate as a white flower. Her eyes were softly brilliant – more glisten than glitter.

He took both her hands. 'Gisela . . .' At the moment that was all he could say.

Gaiety and tenderness met in her smile. A gentle gaiety that brought back memories of Europe and the prewar world. One more war, he thought bitterly, and there will be no one left in the whole world who can smile like that. For an instant, he saw her as a drifting fragment from a lost civilization – broken and still lovely like a mutilated statue from Attica or Lydia.

Then he was sitting beside her on the upholstered bench against the wall and the waiter was setting two cold, bitter Martinis on the table in front of them.

Her glance took in his white tie, slightly yellowed after six years in a bureau drawer.

'Out of uniform – for good?'

'God willing, for ever!' He drank it as a toast, devoutly. 'That's why I chose this place for us tonight.' He looked about at the garish clash of metallic colours that was the latest fad in decoration. 'Could any place be more civilian than the Crane Club?'

'Well . . .' She smiled again. 'That little bar on First Avenue where we used to go was not exactly military.'

'So you do remember?'

'Did you think I would forget?'

They said the rest with their eyes. Then Basil laughed. 'My favourite bar – I admit. Every man in it a character out of Dickens or Saroyan. But hardly the place to celebrate my return from the dead. I'm doing everything I can to recover the past. I've got back my old job as medical assistant to the district attorney, though there's a new district attorney now and a new Mayor. My old place as head of the psychiatric clinic at Knickerbocker Hospital has gone to a friend of mine – fellow I last saw in Scotland named Dunbar. But I've landed the same job at a better hospital – the Murray Hill. The tenants who sub-leased my house for the duration have gone back to Chicago. Juniper and I moved in yesterday. If I can just convince him that I don't want to redecorate, no matter how shabby things look, I shall really begin to believe I'm home again. There's only one thing lacking.'

'And that is?'

'You.'

Faint colour stained her pale cheeks.

'Just why are you teaching at Brereton?' he demanded almost accusingly.

'One must live – whether others see the necessity or not!'

'It's not the place for you. Are you under contract?'

'Until June.'

'And this is November. Break your contract.'

'My dear, really! Are you joking?'

'I've never been more serious. Brereton isn't healthy for you. It isn't even safe.'

'What do you mean?'

'You've been seeing too much of this – what's her name? Faustina Crayle.'

'Oh, my letter!' Gisela laughed. 'I had forgotten all about that. You didn't mention it when we talked on the telephone and made our appointment for this evening. Now I'm here with you, it doesn't seem real.'

'But it will tonight, when you go back to it.'

'It's all over now.'

'Of course. Faustina is gone.'

'You think so?'

'But the people who got her out are still there.'

The waiter was serving sweetbreads. When he had left them alone again, Basil leaned forward. 'Your letter was sketchy. I wish you'd tell me when and how you first noticed anything odd about Miss Crayle.'

'But there wasn't anything odd about Faustina herself,' protested

Gisela. 'The odd thing was the way other people reacted to her.'

'That's the same thing. When did it begin?'

'The first few days.' Gisela was surprised that he took it so seriously.

'And the first incident?'

'I don't remember,' she said ruefully. 'There are so many things to do in a new job. It was my first term as well as hers. I suppose I'd been there about a week when I began to realize she was unpopular. It seemed to start with the servants and spread to the pupils and finally to the other teachers until it amounted to a persecution. Then she was dismissed.'

'Was that all?'

'There were a few incidents after I wrote to you.'

'Tell me.'

She gave him all the details.

'Why did other teachers avoid Miss Crayle?' queried Basil. 'Have you no idea?'

Gisela hesitated. 'I had a curious impression that they were afraid of her. And, of course, you hate what you fear.'

'What had they to fear?'

'Oh, I don't know! The whole thing was – uncanny. Mob spirit, I suppose. And I have the most extraordinary feeling that I've known or read something like this somewhere a long time ago.'

'Perhaps you have. As soon as I finished your letter, I telephoned Brentano's for a copy of Goethe's *Memoirs* in the French edition translated by Madame Carlowitz.'

'I re-read the first volume after Faustina returned it. I couldn't find anything that reminded me of her situation.'

'But you didn't know what you were looking for,' Basil reminded her. 'You don't yet know what Faustina's situation really is.'

A dance band crashed into the latest distortion of music. Gisela sighed. 'How can we talk about anything so intangible in a place like this?'

'Then we'll go some place else,' responded Basil swiftly. 'You don't really like it here, do you?'

'No, but . . .

He had already summoned an astonished waiter to pay the cheque for a dinner they had not eaten.

That was how it came to pass that the humdrum regulars at a neighbourhood bar on First Avenue were bemused that night by the sudden invasion of an exotic couple – foreigners from Fifth or Park. The woman in a long black velvet coat with lapels of flame-coloured silk. The man with a top hat and one of those white scarves just like something in the movies. More polite than Fifth and Park, First Avenue did not stare or whisper. First is nothing if not tolerant. It will even tolerate the undeserving rich if they are quiet and well-behaved.

'This is where we should have come in the first place,' Basil looked nostalgically at walls darkened by age, smoke, and the black dust of the city. 'It hasn't changed at all.'

'The juke box is new,' objected Gisela.

They looked with distaste at an illuminated monster glaring at them through a haze of cigarette smoke.

'Rather like one of those self-lighted fish at the bottom of the sea,' murmured Gisela. Then she surrendered to the spirit of the place. 'Got any nickels?'

'Only if you promise not to play that reindeer thing.'

He gave their usual order – toasted cheese sandwiches and the beer that was almost Pilsener. She came back to the table radiant because she had found the 'Glass Slipper Waltz' from the *Cinderella Suite* composed by Basil's grandfather, Vassily Krasnoy.

'Syncopated, of course. But, even that way, it's wonderful. I don't know how it got there. Everything else was molasses.'

No one else was listening. At the next table, a pair of tramps divided a glass of beer between them and pored over a tabloid someone else had discarded, intent and serious as scholars deciphering a medieval manuscript. Gaunt, hungry, dirty – what had they found in the news of the day to take their minds so completely off their own troubles?

Just then one spoke: 'I tell you, there ain't no cure for dandruff. Science is baffled.'

'Well, it says here . . .' The other began to spell out printed words laboriously. 'First – wash – the – head – thoroughly . . .'

'Page Saroyan!' whispered Gisela. 'The Crane Club can't beat that!'

It was so easy to talk here, and there was so much to talk about that they didn't get back to Faustina until Gisela began to look anxiously at the clock over the bar.

'I hate to think of you going back there.' Basil looked down into his third glass of beer. 'Your Mrs Lightfoot wouldn't ruin the girl's career unless the girl herself was responsible in some way for what happened.'

'You mean Faustina herself was – playing tricks? But how? And why?'

'When Miss Crayle asked if you had heard any gossip about

her, you said: "No". Why was that?'

'I knew people were talking about her, but I didn't know what they were saying. And even if I had – one doesn't repeat gossip to the victim, if the victim is a friend. It's one of the things you can't do. Unwritten law. Like telling a husband his wife is unfaithful.'

'Even when the victim asks for it?'

'Especially when the victim asks for it! No one really wants to see himself as others see him. If people ask, they're really asking to be reassured. Just as no artist or writer ever wants real criticism for the work he shows you. Just praise. Persian kings used to kill the messenger who brought bad news. We'd all like to.'

'I wonder if that was really your feeling,' insisted Basil. 'It could have been that you didn't trust Miss Crayle yourself.'

'Oh, no!' exclaimed Gisela. 'I did trust her and I do now. I'd do anything I could to help her.'

'You're sure?'

'Yes.'

'Then get me some authorization to represent her. I'll go up to Brereton tomorrow and insist on some explanation from Mrs Lightfoot. As a psychiatrist, I'm interested in the rather startling effects of gossip at Brereton.'

'Nonsense! You're trying to keep me out of trouble!'

'Egoist! Only I shouldn't use the word "trouble". I'd say "danger".'

'Why?'

'There's malice in this. It did cost Faustina Crayle her job. Malice, secret and triumphant, is an unholy thing. It might seek a fresh victim.'

'Faustina is staying in New York now. At the Fontainebleau.' Gisela took a visiting card out of her beaded bag. 'If you have a pen or pencil I'll write on this.'

He borrowed a fountain pen from the bartender. 'And now I'll drive you to Grand Central. If you really must make that eleven-ten train.'

'There's a school party at Brereton tomorrow afternoon. Would you like to come?'

'I have to spend the afternoon testifying at an insanity hearing. I'll come to Brereton in the morning.'

'And I have a class in the morning!' Gisela made a small grimace.

'Are you free for dinner Friday evening?'

'That would be perfect. No classes Saturday. So I won't have to hurry back to school.'

The car slid to a stop between First and Second Avenues. The cross street was empty and dark, for the warehouses on either side were shuttered and the only street lamp was far away at the corner. Just then there were no pedestrians. Without a word they turned to each other and their lips met.

At last Gisela moved and he released her. 'I travelled six thousand miles for that,' he said. 'They wanted me to stay in Japan another year or two.'

'I'm glad you didn't,' she answered shakily.

'Are you? Then break that contract with Brereton!'

'I – oh, I don't know!'

'What don't you know?'

'Tonight any woman who wasn't a lunatic or a cripple would seem lovely to you. Tomorrow . . .' She shrugged. 'Don't come any farther. The station's only two blocks away.'

Without answering he let out the clutch. The car moved toward the tinsel lights of Lexington Avenue. At Grand Central he bent his head to kiss her hand. 'I'll be at Brereton tomorrow morning.'

'Tomorrow morning? But you have to see Faustina first!'

'I shall see Miss Crayle tonight.'

CHAPTER FIVE

Since first the Devil threw dice with God
For you, Faustine . . .

The Fontainebleau was a product of the other inflation after the other war. It pretended to be a luxury hotel; actually it was the old-fashioned working-girls' hostel streamlined and gilded. Male guests were not permitted. The bedrooms were narrow cells, scantily furnished. But the building itself was a skyscraper on the fringe of a fashionable neighbourhood with gaudy reception rooms on the first floor, a swimming-pool and squash court in the basement. Its promoters exploited two basic feminine fears – the fear of seeming shabby and the fear of seeming disreputable. But Basil suspected that it was not these commonplace anxieties which had brought Faustina to such a populous, protected place.

As he entered the lobby his mind went back twenty years to the time when he was a young man new to New York calling at the Fontainebleau to see girls he had known at home in Baltimore. Girls whose parents would allow them to work or study in New York only if they promised to stay at this hotel for women.

Nothing had changed. The reception rooms were still glossy with spurious marble and mahogany-finished metal. At this hour they were still animated with girls in wolf or bunny that looked almost like fox or ermine giving good night to artless youths who had taken them to theatre or movies. The naïveté in the blooming faces, unformed mouths, and long knobby wrists made him feel old and wise and weary as he picked up the house telephone and asked for Miss Crayle.

'Yes?'

'My name is Willing – Basil Willing. You don't know me, but I am a friend of Gisela von Hohenems.'

'Oh, yes. I've heard her mention your name.'

'I've just put her on the train back to Brereton. We had dinner together and she told me something about your circumstances. I'd like to talk to you. I might be able to help.'

'That's very kind. Perhaps tomorrow . . .'

'The matter may be more urgent than you realize. I'm downstairs in the lobby now. Is it too late for me to see you tonight?'

'No – no . . . I suppose not. There's a roof garden. If you'll take the express elevator, I'll meet you there. We don't have sitting-rooms and the lobby is always crowded at this time.'

When he reached the roof, he was alone there except for one couple in a far corner. He could just see their faces, two blurred patches of whiteness, and the red embers of their cigarettes. He strolled to the other corner and leaned on the parapet. After dark, light from the streets and the other tall buildings kept the place in an eerie, perpetual twilight. There was a stunted box hedge in a tiled trough and some metal furniture, all gritty with city dust. But the view was breathtaking. Cubic masses of masonry, piled haphazardly against the night sky, shimmering with yellow lights as if a hundred torchlight processions were climbing a hundred Bald Mountains to celebrate some Walpurgis night at the top. It was always hard to realize that such artful splendour was the chance accretion of a city grown too big for its island birth. His feeling toward the Fontainebleau grew a little kindlier. Perhaps it did give something to the girl from Oshkosh that she couldn't get from the third floor back of a brownstone house.

'Dr Willing?'

He liked the voice. Quiet, reserved, with a lapidary clearness in enunciation. He turned and saw a girl nearly his own height, but so slender, with such narrow, stooping shoulders, that she did not seem a big woman. Her simple dress was white or some light shade that looked white in the darkness. Her oval face and fine, floating hair were two tones of biscuit colour, almost as pale as the dress. She led the way to chairs grouped around a low table and they sat down.

'I'll begin by explaining just why I'm here,' said Basil. 'I don't like the sound of the things that have been happening at Brereton. Gisela has gone back there and I'm afraid. For her.'

'For her?' repeated the small, colourless voice. 'I don't see how there could be any – trouble for her.'

He began to be sorry he had agreed to meet Faustina on the roof. It was impossible to see her distinctly in this queer artificial dusk. Tall, attenuated, with straightened flanks and shoulders, pale skin and hair and dress, she seemed flat and insubstantial as a paper doll. And with as little expression.

'Gisela identified herself with you at the school,' he explained. 'A mischief-maker might turn attention to her now that you've gone. She was your only confidante, wasn't she?'

'Yes. I told her everything that happened.'

'Everything?'

If Faustina's colour changed, if her eyes shifted, he could not see them. She sat still in the faint light, apparently composed. Her response was an evasion. 'There's nothing I can add now.' Even her voice was the same – thin, dry, precise, a little pedantic. 'Dr Willing, you're a psychiatrist, aren't you?'

'Yes.'

'Is that why Gisela sent you to see me? Does she think that I was just imagining things when I said people were always watching me? That I'm neurotic or – worse?'

'Miss Crayle, I'll be frank. Gisela didn't think of that. But I did, when she told me your story.'

'And now . . . ?'

'I couldn't tell without a complete psychiatric examination.'

'My mental health has never been questioned,' protested Faustina. 'And my physical health has always been good. I am a little anaemic, but I'm taking iron and vitamin pills for that now. Do you really believe a psychiatric examination is necessary?'

'There's another way to find out, an easier way – if you have the courage.'

'And that is?'

'Let me talk to Mrs Lightfoot on your behalf. She owes you some explanation. She might tell me things she wouldn't tell you.'

'Oh . . .' Faustina was still indistinct in that dreamlike dusk, but now her voice gave her away. Basil could have understood her being hurt or angry after Mrs Lightfoot's high-handed treatment. But why was she afraid?

'Gisela told me you had no family. Is that correct?'

'Yes. There's nobody but Mr Watkins. He was my mother's lawyer. When she died, he became my guardian and trustee.'

'It didn't occur to you to tell him about this?'

'Mr Watkins is an old man, practical and definite. There was nothing definite to tell him except that I'd been dismissed without explanation. I – I just couldn't tell a man like that.'

'Either he or I should see Mrs Lightfoot for you.'

'I'd rather you did.'

'It's going to be an ordeal for you. Can you face it? Now? You should. Your whole future will depend on it.'

'Very well.' Her voice was still frightened, but a note of recklessness had come into it – the last, desperate boldness of the timid when they are trapped. 'I'll face it. Now.'

'Good girl. I'll see her tomorrow,' he went on, briskly. 'You'll be here the next few days?'

'Yes. I – I want a chance to get my breath.'

'And then?'

'If I can't find another job, I'll go to New Jersey. My mother left me a seaside cottage at Brightsea. I can hole up there for the winter.'

'I hope you won't think me impertinent, but – what about finances?'

'I have six months' salary from Mrs Lightfoot and some savings. Altogether enough to last six or eight months if I'm careful.'

'That's all?'

'I own the cottage at Brightsea. And I will inherit some other things of my mother's on my thirtieth birthday. Jewels. Mostly trinkets, I suppose, though Mr Watkins says there are a few good stones. Mr Watkins would advance money on the strength of them if I needed cash before next fall. I'll be thirty next October.'

'Have you any idea why you didn't inherit the other things at the same time you inherited the cottage?'

'The cottage isn't very valuable, so she left it to me outright and I came into ownership automatically when I came of age. But those few good jewels are the only capital I'll ever have, and my mother was afraid I'd sell them and squander the money if I inherited them when I was too young to understand the value of security. You see, she died when I was only seven years old. She left just enough money to put me through school and college. During vacations Mr Watkins sent me to summer camps at his own expense, because he had no wife or children of his own and he really didn't know what else to do with me.'

'There were no aunts or cousins on either side?'

'No. I really know very little about my family, Dr Willing. I can just remember my mother as a beautiful woman with auburn hair in a sealskin sacque with white kid gloves and violets pinned to her muff. And I have another mental picture of her all in white with a long-handled sunshade of embroidered white linen. I don't remember my father at all, so he must have died when I was a baby. I've wondered quite a lot about his relatives.' Her voice grew wistful. 'I always knew mother was alone in the world, but it did seem odd that father didn't have any relatives either. Once or twice I've asked Mr Watkins, but he always says, very firmly, that there isn't anybody left on either side and I must try to get used to the idea of being alone.'

'After I've seen Mrs Lightfoot I may wish to talk to this Mr Watkins. How can I reach him?'

'He has an office at the corner of Broad and Wall.'

Basil was surprised. 'Not Septimus Watkins?' He had been assuming that 'Mr Watkins' was some obscure legal hack with a little office on a side street. There was nothing about Faustina to suggest that her mother's lawyer had been one of the most celebrated legal lights of his generation.

'Yes. That's his name. And if you really wish to see him personally, you'll have to get up early.' Faustina smiled tentatively, as if her facial muscles were unaccustomed to the expression. 'He keeps very peculiar office hours – from six to seven in the morning.'

'Really?' He was sure she must be mistaken. It would be simple to call Watkins's secretary for an appointment at a more reasonable hour if he decided to see the man.

Basil rose. 'I'm glad you're going to face the issue squarely.'

She walked across the terrace with him to the elevator.

'You'll call me as soon as you get back to New York?'

'Of course.' He looked down at her thoughtfully. 'There's one more thing I'd like to ask you. How did you happen to borrow the first volume of Gisela's Goethe *Memoirs*? Any special reason?'

'No. I've always been interested in Goethe.'

Psychiatric experience had taught him to recognize the unskilful liar. But this was no time to accuse her. He must win her confidence first. The fact that she told her little lie so awkwardly impressed him. Basically she was honest. He couldn't see her as the centre of an elaborate hoax or intrigue.

'Dr Willing . . .' Her voice died away.

'Yes.'

She took a deeper breath and looked up at him. 'No matter what Mrs Lightfoot says tomorrow – please believe in my good faith, won't you?'

'I'm going there to represent your interests,' he answered gravely. 'Is there anything else you wish to tell me before I go?'

The elevator door clanged open. Her eyes winced from the sudden, bright light as from a blow. For the first time he saw her face clearly – a thin, anaemic face with a mild expression. He would have said an innocent face if it had not been so ravaged with doubt and insecurity.

'No. Not now,' she whispered. 'But – I'd like to see you again as soon as you get back.'

'I'll call you tomorrow evening. You're taking this elevator?'

'No. It's an express and I'm on the sixteenth floor. Good night and – thank you.'

As the elevator plunged to the ground floor, he wondered what she might have said if its coming had been delayed a moment longer . . .

Next morning, at half past nine, Basil asked his secretary at the clinic to call Septimus Watkins's office and discover the best hour for an appointment with the head of the firm. She put down the telephone and looked at Basil with a dazed expression. 'His secretary says Mr Watkins does not make appointments.'

Irritably, Basil took the telephone himself and repeated the question. A man's voice answered in singsong, as if this were ritual: 'Mr Watkins does not make appointments.'

'But . . .'

'You may see him any morning you wish, sir, between six and seven.'

'Are you joking?' demanded Basil indignantly. 'You don't even know who I am.'

'No, sir.' The secretary was as remotely civil as an English man-servant. 'It's an old rule of this office. Mr Watkins will see anyone between six and seven in the morning without appointment.'

Basil put down the telephone in disgust and went downstairs to his car.

It took him two hours' steady driving to reach Brereton. He

slowed as he passed through the iron gates, casting an inquisitive eye over house and grounds. The lawns and flower beds were as neat as those around a prison. The house itself was an ugly barracks of red brick that looked brown in the grim light sifting through November clouds.

His ring was answered by a maid in blue cambray. Her dull eyes quickened at the unexpected sight of a male visitor.

'Is Mrs Lightfoot at home?'

'Is she expecting you, sir?'

'No, but I think she'll see me, if you'll take her my card.'

The girl's lips moved silently as she read: _Dr Basil Willing, Medical Assistant to the District Attorney of New York County._ For a moment she looked at him with the unembarrassed greed of the natural-born autograph hunter. Then she remembered her training.

'Please come inside, sir. I'll see if Mrs Lightfoot is at home.'

CHAPTER SIX

Your naked, newborn soul their stake
Stood blind between;
God said: 'Let him that wins her take
And keep Faustine.'

'Dr Willing?' Mrs Lightfoot stood beside her desk in the study. She was holding Basil's card fastidiously between thumb and forefinger. 'This is Connecticut, not New York. And I fail to see how anything at Brereton can interest a district attorney or his medical assistant.'

'That happened to be the only card I had with me,' answered Basil. 'My job with the district attorney is only one phase of my work. Primarily I'm a psychiatrist.'

The word 'psychiatrist' seemed to disturb Mrs Lightfoot as much as the words 'district attorney'.

'I believe you know one of my teachers, Miss von Hohenems. I seem to remember a telephone call.'

'It was Miss von Hohenems who introduced me to Faustina Crayle.'

Mrs Lightfoot sighed elaborately. 'Don't tell me you are going to revive that unhappy business!' It was a masterly display of restrained indignation. 'That would be most unfair to everyone concerned – including Miss Crayle herself.'

'Do you think it fair to dismiss a teacher without a character when you are apparently unable to make any charge against her?'

'Please sit down, Dr Willing.' Mrs Lightfoot resumed her own seat behind the desk. The hands she clasped above the blotter were plump as a child's, but he saw maturity and character in the stubby profile outlined against a curtain of rose-red behind her chair. Naturally she would assess most things in relation to the prosperity of her school. Her dignity was a professional asset carefully cultivated. Underneath she was restless, intelligent, aggressive. She might not be too scrupulous if her interests were threatened.

She was studying him as deliberately as he studied her. A slight puckering of her brow told him that he puzzled her. No doubt she expected anyone connected with the county administration of New York to be a ready-made political type, Tammany Irish, or Fusion Italian. But he was not a type – a man she could 'place' after a few words and gestures. He was an individual full of contradictions who must baffle and probably annoy such a practised appraiser of worldly values.

'You say I dismissed Miss Crayle without making any charge against her,' resumed Mrs Lightfoot. 'That is true. I have not even investigated the rather peculiar charges that were brought against her by others.'

'Why not?'

'I have no vulgar curiosity.'

'Vulgar?' Basil smiled. 'Curiosity is the tap root of an intellectual life, the most valuable of our simian traits.'

Mrs Lightfoot returned his smile, a little reluctantly. 'Let me try to make my meaning clearer. Even if the extraordinary stories told about Miss Crayle were all lies or hallucinations, it makes no difference to me. For the effect on the school would be the same as if the stories were true, and that alone concerns me.'

'But it does make a difference to Miss Crayle. Why wasn't she told about these stories? Surely she deserved that much consideration!'

'In most cases, yes. In this case, the sooner the whole thing is forgotten, the better for everyone involved.' Mrs Lightfoot could be blunt when necessary. 'Just what do you want, Dr Willing?'

He matched her with equal bluntness. 'To know why Miss Crayle was dismissed. You gave her six months' salary for five weeks' work. The incentive must have been powerful.'

'It was. Did Miss Crayle herself give you no hint of the – incentive?'

'How could she? She had no idea what it was.'

'I was never sure . . .' Mrs Lightfoot looked down at the rose-wood desk.

'Of what?'

'Of whether Miss Crayle herself knew what was going on at Brereton – or not. Sometimes I thought that she must know. Even that she might be engineering the whole thing herself, for whatever reason. At other times, I thought she was a victim of forces outside her own knowledge and control.'

'Forces?' Basil shifted his point of attack. 'That's pretty vague. Of course, there are shadowy things you might suspect and be unable to prove. They range all the way from alcoholism to communism. In such cases you'd send Miss Crayle away, because you couldn't afford to take a chance, but you wouldn't tell her why, because she might sue for libel if you accused her without proof.

That's the sort of thing people are going to say when they hear Miss Crayle was dismissed without explanation. It isn't going to be nice for your school, either.'

She lifted her eyes. 'It was nothing of that sort.' The bright, hard enamel of her manner had cracked. She was profoundly disturbed. She spoke with great bitterness. 'I suppose I shall have to tell you.'

'Why are you afraid to tell me?' he asked, more gently.

Her response startled him. 'Because you won't believe me.' She sighed. 'I hardly believe it myself. And yet – you would better hear the story from some of the eye-witnesses. Then you won't think I'm inventing. It won't take long as there are only four witnesses left. The other seven have gone.' She pressed a bell beside her hand on the desk. 'There's one thing I'd like to make clear before Arlene comes. I still have no idea what the truth is about Faustina Crayle. She may, or she may not, have been the cause of all that happened here. But this I do know: she was the occasion – the focus of all the – unpleasantness. Now she's gone, it's stopped. That's why she had to go. And that's why I shall not take her back, no matter how you urge me or appeal to my compassion. And . . .'

She was interrupted by a knock on the door. She raised her voice: 'Come in!'

The door opened. The maid who had answered the doorbell stood on the threshold. Basil examined her with greater attention this time. Her body was bulky, shapeless; her face, a heavy lump of flesh that looked as if it had been moulded hastily into a semblance of human features by an unskilful hand. The blue cambray was unbecoming – high-necked, long-sleeved, full-skirted. Mrs Lightfoot had won the battle for low heels, apron, and cap, but

Arlene had gained two points for herself – lipstick and flesh-coloured stockings.

'You rang, ma'am?'

'Yes. Dr Willing, this is our second housemaid, Arlene Murphy. Come in and shut the door, Arlene. Will you please repeat to Dr Willing exactly what you told me about Miss Crayle?'

'You said not to tell anybody.'

'I'm releasing you from that promise, just this once.'

Arlene turned curious eyes on Basil. The hair that straggled from a bun at the nape of her neck was abundant, but she had no eyebrows. This gave her face a singularly naked look. Some glandular deficiency, he suspected. And her breathing through the mouth suggested sinus or adenoids. That meant poverty and neglect during childhood. Did her sullen manner spring from resentment of the Brereton girls, whose skin and teeth and hair were so eloquent of the care that wealth and intelligence can give the young? Did she ever eye the fur coats in their closets with envy or finger their textbooks with resentment? It would be only human, he thought, if you were a girl the same age, dusting and bed-making among other girls whose lives were so much fuller than your own . . .

'The first time was a month ago – just two weeks after school opened,' said Arlene. 'I was upstairs, turning down beds for the night. When I got through, I started down the back stairs. I was on my way to the drawing-room to light the fire and empty the scrap-baskets. I could have saved two minutes by using the front stairs, only Mrs Lightfoot says we have to use the back stairs, so I did.'

Mrs Lightfoot ignored the sulky glance that punctuated this.

'It was getting dark,' went on Arlene. 'But it was still light enough to see the steps. You know. Dim, but just too early to turn the lights on. Those back stairs are walled in, but there are two windows. They curve around twice – the stairs, I mean, not the windows.' Her breathless giggle came and went swiftly as a nervous twitch, leaving her face blank. 'It was then . . .' She paused to swallow. Basil saw that her hands were trembling. 'It was then that I saw Miss Crayle, coming up the stairs toward me.'

'Yes?' Basil tried to put her at ease.

But Arlene began to pleat her apron between her fingers. 'I didn't think anything of it then. Except that it was funny, her using the back stairs instead of the front. I came on her quite sudden, rounding the first curve. I stopped and stood against the wall to let her pass, and I said: "Good evening, Miss." Because I always liked her. She wasn't stuck up, like some of the others. But this time, she didn't answer. She didn't even look at me. She just went on up to the second floor. That was kind of queer, because she was always real nice to everybody – even to me. Still, I didn't think much about it. I went on down into the kitchen and' – once more, Arlene paused to swallow – 'there was Miss Crayle.'

The hands on her apron were still. Her eyes searched Basil's face. 'Honest to God, sir, she couldn't have got back to the kitchen by way of the upstairs hall and the front stairs and the dining-room in the little time it took me to finish going down the back stairs to the kitchen. She just couldn't – even if she'd run all the way. I just stood there, stock-still, staring at her. I felt as if I was going nuts. Then as I got my breath, I said, "Lord, Miss. You sure did give me a turn." She looked surprised and said, "I? What do you mean?" I said: "I could've sworn I passed you on the back stairs just now, going up when I was coming down." She said: "You must have been mistaken, Arlene. I've been outdoors sketching since three o'clock. I only came into the house a moment ago and I haven't been upstairs yet."

'Then cook had to put in her two cents' worth. "That's right," says she. "Miss Crayle has been here with me ever since she came in from outside."

'I said, "But I did see you, Miss Crayle. Going up the stairs as I came down just two seconds ago." Miss Crayle said: "It must have been somebody else wearing a coat like mine."

'I said, "Excuse me, miss, but it wasn't. I seen – saw your face."

'Cook is a great one for telling us to mind our manners, and she said, "That'll do, Arlene. I've told you before you must not contradict people." So – I kept my mouth shut.'

'What was Miss Crayle doing in the kitchen?' asked Basil.

'She had her easel and paintbox and she was washing her brushes at the sink. She'd been outdoors sketching those little purple flowers that come out in the fall.'

'Were the two figures dressed in exactly the same way? The one on the back stairs and the one in the kitchen?'

'Yes, sir. As like as two peas. Brown felt hat and bluish-grey coat. Covert, I think they call it. Too plain for me. No fur. No style at all. And brown shoes. The sort with no tongues and criss-cross laces that they call "gillies".'

'Had the hat a brim?'

'Uh-huh. I mean, yes. What you might call, a slouch hat. All sloppy.'

Basil silently thanked God that the dullest woman had a keen eye for another woman's clothes. 'Did you see Miss Crayle's face distinctly on the stairs?'

'Well, I did and I didn't. I wasn't looking at her particular. No reason why I should. And the hat brim was down over her eyes. But I saw her mouth and chin as clear as clear when she went by me. I'd still swear it was her, but well – you know how it is, sir. Something like that happens once or even twice and you think: What the – I mean, oh, well, gee, I must have been mistaken. Leastways, that's what you think if nothing more happens.'

'And something more did happen?'

'That was just the beginning! Pretty soon the other maids were telling the same sort of stories about Miss Crayle. Two of them left, and it got so I used to run if I had to go up the back stairs alone or down a dark hall at night. Why, the very day Miss Crayle left – two days ago – she was in the kitchen, fixing some flowers there, and Miss Aitchison was just coming in the back door with Miss von Hohenems as I came down the back stairs. I heard Miss Crayle say to Miss Aitchison, "I've been in the cutting garden for the last half-hour. " And Miss Aitchison answered in a queer voice: "I thought I saw your face at an upstairs window just now." It was such a jolt to me, I dropped the tray I was carrying. You see, I had just been upstairs, turning down beds for the night again. I hadn't seen anybody, but I had heard steps and . . .'

'Dr Willing is interested only in what you actually saw, Arlene,' interpolated Mrs Lightfoot.

'And I bet he doesn't believe me.' Arlene's eyes slid sideways toward Basil. 'Mrs Lightfoot didn't at first. Cook must've told her about that first time, because she questioned me a week later. Then she wanted me to go to a doctor.'

'There was always the possibility of hallucination rooted in some physical cause,' explained Mrs Lightfoot, carefully.

'I been to a doctor.' Arlene looked full at Basil. 'He couldn't find nothing wrong.'

'Arlene went to her family doctor. A general practitioner, in a small town. Hardly competent to diagnose a thing like this. I offered to pay expenses if she'd go to a psychiatrist in New York, but she refused.'

'I wouldn't go within fifty miles of one of them psycho – what-is-its!' cried Arlene. 'I seen one in the movies,' she added darkly.

Basil looked quizzically at Mrs Lightfoot. She spoke sharply. 'That's enough, Arlene. You understand that you are not to repeat what you have just told us to anyone else? And you are not to discuss Dr Willing's visit, either. And now – please ask Miss Vining and Miss Chase to come to my study immediately.'

'Yes, ma'am.' Once more Arlene's face was closed and sullen. She went out, stepping softly, closing the door quietly as she had been trained to do.

'Well?' Mrs Lightfoot looked at Basil defiantly. 'Not what you expected, I imagine?'

'Hardly. But I'm beginning to understand – several things.' His smile was thoughtful. 'Goethe. Volume One of the *Memoirs*. The grey suit with gilt edging. Emilie Sagée and *The Tale of Tod Lapraik*. The *doppelgänger* of the Germans. The *eidolon* of the Greeks. The *ka* of the Egyptians. The *fetch* of English folklore. The *gavar vore* of the Celts. You enter a room, a street, a country road. You see a figure ahead of you, solid, three-dimensional, brightly coloured. Moving and obeying all the laws of optics. Its clothing and posture is vaguely familiar. You hurry toward the figure for a closer view. It turns its head and – you are looking at yourself. Or rather a perfect mirror-image of yourself only – there is no mirror. So, you know it is your double. And that frightens you, for tradition tells you that he who sees his own double is about to die . . .'

'As a psychiatrist, you naturally know the history of the subject,' replied Mrs Lightfoot. 'I have become acquainted with it only in the last few days. The tradition of these doubles is psychologically – curious.'

'Too curious to be encouraged in a girls' school?'

'Exactly.' Mrs Lightfoot fingered the pens in the copper pentray. 'Sometimes . . . I wonder if such visions are purely subjective or if somehow under certain unknown conditions, some portion of the atmosphere could act as a mirror. Roughly analogous to the mirage which I believe is a double of earth or sky reflected by layers of warm air.'

Basil looked at her intently. 'Do you know of anyone who had a grudge against Miss Crayle?'

'No.' Mrs Lightfoot raised startled eyes. 'Why do you ask?'

'Traditionally, the double is always associated with death, whether it is seen by oneself or others. So the appearance of Miss Crayle's double, however contrived, might be a symbolic intimation of Miss Crayle's death. Psychologically on the same plane as a threatening anonymous letter.' Basil was looking at her intently. 'Miss Crayle was not popular here, but – did anyone actually hate her?'

Before Mrs Lightfoot could answer, a knock fell on the door.

CHAPTER SEVEN

The die rang sideways as it fell,
Rang cracked and thin,
Like a man's laughter heard in Hell
Far down, Faustine.

Meg and Beth entered the study decorously and curtseyed to Basil when Mrs Lightfoot introduced him.

Meg was fresh as a pink rose at sunrise, but Basil saw a nervous temperament in the sensitive curve of her lips. Even in repose, her mouth seemed to quiver on the edge of tears or laughter. Beth was the perfect foil, her light-brown hair cut straight as a Dutch peasant boy's, her narrow face peppered with freckles.

The two listened gravely as Mrs Lightfoot explained. 'Both of you promised me not to repeat the incident that occurred in the writing-room when Miss Crayle was here. I'm going to release you from that promise just this once. I want you to tell Dr Willing everything that happened as nearly as you can recall it.'

'It was last Tuesday . . .'

'Meg and I were in the writing-room . . .'

Both girls stopped short and looked at each other.

'Margaret, suppose you tell Dr Willing what happened,' said Mrs Lightfoot. 'Elizabeth may correct you if you make any mistake.'

'Yes, Mrs Lightfoot.'

Obviously Meg enjoyed being the centre of the stage. There was a touch of envy in Beth's sidelong glance at her friend.

'We two were alone in the writing-room on the ground floor,' began Meg.

'It's a little room just off the library,' Beth explained to Basil. 'With pens and notepaper.'

'And a mailbox,' added Meg. 'Not a real post-office box, you know. Just one that belongs to the school. I was writing my brother, Raymond, and Beth was writing her mother. All the other girls were out on the bridle path and most of the teachers. It was pretty warm for November. The window was open and the sun was shining bright as could be on the lawn that slopes down to the creek.'

'I could smell chrysanthemums outside the window,' chimed in Beth. 'Just as if they were cooking in the sun.'

'She was just outside the window – Miss Crayle,' went on Meg. 'I could see her plainly. She had her easel set up in the middle of the lawn and she was sketching in watercolours. She was wearing a blue coat and brown hat. She had her paintbox at her feet and a small palette in her left hand. She was quite good at watercolours. Better than she was at oils. Whenever I couldn't think what to put in my letter, I'd look up and watch the quick way she handled her brush. You know – mixing colours on the palette one minute, daubing them on paper the next.'

'Quick?' interrupted Beth.

'She was quick then,' retorted Meg.

'That's so, but – you've forgotten the armchair.'

'What armchair? Oh, the blue one.' Meg turned back to Basil. 'There's an armchair in the hall just outside that room with a slipcover in blue twill. You can see it through the doorway into the hall. We used to call it "Miss Crayle's chair" because she sat there so often. She liked the view of the garden from the hall window.'

'I was rather expecting her to come in and sit there when she was through painting,' added Beth. 'And then it happened.' Her voice faded, suddenly shy.

'What happened?' asked Basil, patiently.

'Mrs Lightfoot didn't tell you?' Meg, for all her natural vivacity, was stricken dumb. It was Beth who took up the tale now, with the aplomb of a grown woman.

'I looked up and saw that Miss Crayle had come into the hall without my hearing her. She was sitting in the blue armchair with her hands loose in her lap and her head resting against the back, as if she were tired. Her eyes were open but they looked – far away.'

'Unfocused?' suggested Basil.

'Yes, I guess that's what I mean.'

'You "suppose", Beth, you don't "guess",' murmured Mrs Lightfoot.

'She was still wearing the blue coat and brown hat,' continued Beth. 'But she hadn't brought her paintbrush or palette with her. She didn't look at me or speak. She didn't seem to notice me at all. She just sat there, quietly, without moving. So I went on writing. After a while, I looked up again. She was still in the armchair, but that time I happened to look out of the window and . . .' Beth lost her nerve. 'You tell him, Meg.'

'He – he won't believe me,' demurred Meg.

'Try me,' suggested Basil. As she hesitated, he went on, 'Miss Crayle was still sketching outside the window?'

'How did you know?' Meg looked at Basil quickly. 'Oh, I

suppose Mrs Lightfoot told you that much. You see, I heard Beth gasp. So I looked up, too. Beth's face was horribly white. She was staring at the two Miss Crayles – one in the armchair in the house with us, the other on the lawn outside the window.'

'Was there any difference between the two figures?' asked Basil.

'The one in the chair wasn't moving at all. The one outside the window was moving, only . . .' Meg's voice trailed.

'Only what?'

'You remember my telling you how quickly she had been handling her brush. It really darted here and there, like a bird pecking with its beak.'

'Yes.'

'Well, after we saw the figure in the chair, the other figure outside the window was – slower. Every movement was slow and sort of heavy, as if she were terribly tired or sleepy.'

'She made me think of a sleepwalker,' put in Beth.

Basil recalled the same curious detail in Gisela's version of the incident. And Gisela was a witness he trusted – a witness who had not seen the second figure or even heard about it . . .

'How far was each figure from where you were sitting?' he asked.

'The one on the lawn must have been a good forty feet away,' replied Beth, promptly. 'I know that lawn is sixty feet from the window to the creek and she was in the middle. The one in the chair was about thirty feet, I gue—suppose. The writing-room is long and narrow and the hall itself is wide.'

'You said there was bright sunlight on the lawn. What sort of light was there in the hall?'

'We were writing by daylight,' answered Meg. 'It was about

three o'clock, and the light hadn't begun to fade. But that side of the house gets the afternoon sun, so the venetian blinds were half closed and that did make the hall seem a little dimmer than it actually was. Partly because it was so much brighter outside.'

'How long did you see this second figure in the armchair?'

'It must have been at least five minutes,' mused Meg.

'Time is hard to estimate. Did you look at a watch or clock?'

'No. But I'm sure several minutes went by after we both saw it.'

'It was pretty awful.' Beth's voice rose in pitch. 'Sitting there, just the two of us, alone with that – thing in the armchair. And the real Miss Crayle outside the window painting that slow, awful way.'

'Afterward we thought of all sorts of things we might have done,' said Meg. 'Like going out into the hall and trying to touch the one in the armchair. Or calling to Miss Crayle from the window and waking her up from that trance or whatever it was. But while it's happening, you just don't think of those things. You're too scared . . .

'I sat there and told myself it wasn't happening. Only – it was. I tried closing my eyes. When I opened them again, it was still there with us. I kept thinking: *This can't go on for ever. It's got to stop* . . . Maybe it only lasted a minute or so, but it seemed like a hundred years. Then the one in the chair got up and went down the hall without making a sound. It seemed to melt into the shadows at the far end, by the dining-room door, and disappear. That was when Beth screamed and fainted and Miss von Hohenems came running in from the library.'

'When I came to, she was just as usual,' added Beth. 'Miss Crayle, I mean. She moved quickly. And she spoke as if she didn't know what had happened.'

'Did you see the face of the figure in the chair?'

'Oh, yes,' insisted Beth. 'It was Miss Crayle's face, Dr Willing. No doubt in the world about that.'

'Was this your first experience of anything – peculiar about Miss Crayle?'

The two little girls looked at each other. 'Well . . .' Beth paused.

Meg was more glib. 'We had heard stories. This was the first thing we actually saw ourselves.'

'What sort of stories?' queried Basil.

'We – ell . . .' resumed Beth. 'They said you were always seeing Miss Crayle in places where she couldn't possibly be. I mean, you'd see her in one place and then, a moment later, in another place that she couldn't have got to so quickly unless she had passed you on the way, only – she hadn't passed you. At first, people thought it was just a mistake. I mean, they thought you'd mistaken someone else for Miss Crayle in one of the places or you'd overestimated the time it took to get from one place to another. If it had only happened once or even twice, that's what everyone would have thought. But when it happened five or six times and always with Miss Crayle, never with anyone else, then people began to whisper that maybe there was something – odd about Miss Crayle herself.'

'Odd?' repeated Basil. 'In what way?'

Meg's beautiful mouth quivered as she took up the cudgels for Beth. 'She's afraid to say what she means, Dr Willing. She's afraid you'll laugh.'

'I never felt less like laughing,' he assured her with sincerity.

'It seems that things like this have happened before,' ventured Beth. 'Not often, of course. But they have happened. People are always afraid to talk about it because they know that no one will believe them. You have to see a thing like that to believe in it. So they usually keep quiet. But years ago I had a Highland Scottish nursemaid who told me about one of these doubles that was seen in the old country, just before a man died. She called it the *gavar vore*. I had forgotten all about it until this happened with Miss Crayle. Then it all came back to me and I told Meg.'

'And soon it was all over the school,' added Mrs Lightfoot. 'Pupils, servants, even some of the teachers – presumably educated women . . .' She shrugged. 'Unless Dr Willing has further questions, you may go now.'

Basil shook his head.

Meg and Beth were looking at him, their eyes full of questions they dared not ask in Mrs Lightfoot's presence. When Basil opened the door for them, they smiled and chanted demurely: 'Good afternoon, Dr Willing!'

He closed the door and turned to look at Mrs Lightfoot.

'Well?' she said wearily. 'Was a practical woman ever confronted with a more fantastic problem? Yet it had its practical side. You may imagine the effect on parents when distorted versions of the stories began to filter back to them through letters home. Five girls have been withdrawn from Brereton already.'

'You said that seven eyewitnesses had gone?'

'Besides the five girls, there were two maids who left without giving notice. Others will follow their example and more pupils will be removed unless the talk is stopped at once. That's why Miss Crayle had to go.

'Of course it doesn't occur to any of these parents that the stories about Miss Crayle are true. They regard the whole affair as an adolescent outburst of superstitious hysteria – a serious reflection on the school's ability to interest girls in normal work and play.'

'Margaret and Elizabeth are still here. Didn't they write their parents?'

'Margaret has no parents – only a brother. A rather light-hearted young man of twenty-four who doesn't take his duties as guardian too seriously. Elizabeth's parents are divorced. Her mother is occupied chiefly in nagging the courts to increase her alimony, while the father is the mainstay and support of Fifty-second Street night clubs. Neither is greatly concerned with Elizabeth. She's been a pupil here since her ninth year. Margaret only came to us this fall. She had been going to a day school in New York.'

Basil remained standing, one hand on the mantelpiece. 'Did anyone else still in the school actually see Miss Crayle's double close enough for a positive identification? Besides two girls about thirteen and a housemaid of seventeen or eighteen?'

Mrs Lightfoot caught the implication. 'I mentioned a fourth eyewitness. There was one – middle-aged, sober, reasonably observant, and sceptical.'

'And that was . . . ?'

'Myself.'

Basil's hand fell to his side. 'You're serious?'

'Entirely so. Do sit down again. And smoke, if you like.' She went on in a calm, narrative voice:

'It happened just as Miss Crayle was leaving. I had a dinner engagement outside the school that evening. I finished dressing about six o'clock and came out of my room wearing a wrap and gloves. A pair of sconces are always lighted in the upper hall at that hour. Each has a hundred-watt bulb under a small parchment shade and the light they cast extends to the first landing of the front stairs. Below that landing, the stairs were quite dark on this particular evening, for Arlene had neglected to turn on the lights in the lower hall.

'I started down the stairs with one hand on the balustrade, moving rather slowly because my dress had a long, full skirt. As I reached the first landing, someone, in greater haste than I, brushed past me without a word of apology and I saw that it was Miss Crayle.

'I was first aware of her presence before I saw her. She didn't actually jostle me, but I felt the draughty displacement of air that you feel when anyone passes close to you at a rapid pace.

'I didn't see her face as she passed. Once below me, she didn't look around. But I recognized her back – her figure and carriage and clothes. She was wearing her brown hat and her blue covert coat – the only outdoor clothes she had, except a winter coat, still in storage.

'I was annoyed at her rudeness. She had some reason to be angry with me, but nothing is more contemptible than expressing anger by bad manners. I stood still and raised my voice. I made it as crisp and peremptory as I could. And I'm rather good at that. You can't run a school without learning the tricks of authority. I called out:

' "Miss Crayle!"

'The answer came promptly: "Yes, Mrs Lightfoot?"

'But, Dr Willing, that answering voice, Miss Crayle's voice, came from the upstairs hall, above me, though, at that very moment, I could still see Miss Crayle's back moving into the shadows of the lower hall, below me.

'I shrank back against the balustrade – and I do not shrink easily. At that spot, by turning my head quickly, I could look from the bottom to the top of the stairs in an instant. I looked up. Faustina Crayle was standing at the top of the stairs in the full light of the upper hall, wearing her brown hat and blue coat. Her eyes, bright with life and intelligence, looked into mine and she spoke again: "You called me?" There was no mistaking her. She was Faustina Crayle. But – what was it that had hurried past me so brusquely on the stairs, leaving such a vivid impression of rushing air? I looked down again. There was nothing in the lower hall then – nothing but shadows.

'I tried to pull my shaken mind into some sort of coherent whole. I said: "How long have you been standing there?" Even to myself, my voice sounded unnatural.

'She answered: "Only a moment. I was in such a hurry that I had an impulse to slip past you on the stairs. But, of course, I didn't. That would have been awfully rude."

'So she had had an unrealized impulse to pass me on the stairs ... It's hard to explain why that troubled me so much, Dr Willing, but it did. For one thing I remembered how often a sleepwalker will carry out in his sleep an impulse which he has previously suppressed in his waking state. I assure you it took all the nerve I had to go on down those stairs into the shadows below. Of course there was no one there – nothing – except Arlene, whom I could see coming through the dining-room from the kitchen to light the lamps in the drawing-room and the hall. I asked her if she had seen anyone else. She said no. Yet there were only two ways anyone preceding me down the stairs could have left the lower hall – by the drawing-room or by the front door. And I had only taken my eyes off that door for a few seconds, when I was looking up at Miss Crayle.'

Basil pondered. 'Could Arlene . . . ?' He left the question pendant in mid-air.

'Impossible. She had just left the cook in the kitchen at that moment.'

'You spoke of a draughty sensation when the double passed. Was there any sound? A swish of air? Or a rustle of clothing?'

'No sound at all.'

'Footfalls?'

'No. But the stair carpet is thick and soft.'

'Every human body carries some faint odour or combination of odours,' Basil mused aloud. 'Face powder, lipstick, hair tonic, permanent-wave lotion, or shaving lotion. Iodine or some other medicine. The breath odours – food, wine, tobacco. And the clothing odours – mothballs, shoe polish, dry cleaning fluid, Russian leather, Harris tweed. Finally there are those body odours that soap advertisements worry us about. You are one of the witnesses who were close to the double. Did you notice any odour, however faint or fleeting?'

Mrs Lightfoot shook her head emphatically. 'There was no odour, Dr Willing. Unless I missed it.'

'I doubt that.' He glanced toward a row of flowerpots on the window-sill. 'Only a woman with keen senses would enjoy fragrances as delicate as rose geranium and lemon verbena.'

Mrs Lightfoot smiled. 'I even use lemon verbena on my hand-kerchief. My one vice. But a French firm puts out an essence of *verveine* I can't resist. It's supposed to be an after-shaving lotion for men, so I'm probably the only woman in the world who uses it.'

'Did Miss Crayle use any perfume habitually?'

'Lavender. She always used it on her handkerchief.'

'No essence of lavender about the double?'

'No.' Mrs Lightfoot spoke ironically. 'You wouldn't expect a reflection in a mirror to have any odour, would you? Or a mirage?'

Basil drew on his cigarette. 'What is your own explanation of this?'

Mrs Lightfoot's smile died on her lips. 'I see just three possibilities. First, Faustina Crayle may have been a deliberate trickster. If so, how did she create the illusion of her double? And why? She gained nothing. On the contrary, it cost her a good job. Second, Miss Crayle may have been an unconscious trickster, a split personality with impulses to amaze and frighten people that she could not control because she was not aware of them herself. Impulses that her secondary personality carried out in a sort of sleepwalking state without her primary, conscious personality knowing anything about it. That has happened, hasn't it?'

'There are records of such cases in Janet and Prince,' admitted Basil. 'And it would explain her apparently sincere bewilderment when you got rid of her.'

'It answers the question: Why?' agreed Mrs Lightfoot. 'But it leaves unanswered the other question: How? How could she make two little girls believe she was sitting in a chair indoors when she was actually outdoors sketching in watercolours?'

'And your third possibility?'

Mrs Lightfoot looked at him directly. 'In sleepwalking, hypnosis, or split personality, the primary, conscious personality is submerged in sleep while the unconscious secondary personality takes over the body, and often performs acts that were inhibited in the waking state. Suppose that uncensored autonomous action of the unconscious mind could be pushed a little further? Margaret and Elizabeth say that Faustina Crayle moved sleepily when the double appeared. Apparently I myself saw the double carry out an impulse which the real Miss Crayle had suppressed. Just as if this so-called double were a visible projection of Miss Crayle's sub conscious mind . . .

'You see what I mean? Suppose that an unconscious mind could gather unto itself enough vital energy to project some purely visual image or reflection of itself on the air? Perhaps through some form of refracted radiation? A dream-form that was visible to others as well as to the dreamer – visible but not material. Reflections in a mirror are visible but not material. So are rainbows and mirages. So visible that all three can be photographed. But they cannot be touched, they have no third dimension, and they make no sound. They do not exist in normal terms of space-time . . . As you move the sight of them moves with you. In something the same way, no one has ever touched this double or heard any sound it made. It is merely seen.'

'So you believe in it?' asked Basil.

'I am a modern woman, Dr Willing. That means I believe in nothing. I was born without faith in religion and I have lost my faith in science. I don't understand the theories of Messrs Planck and Einstein. But I grasp enough to realize that the world of matter may be a world of appearances – not a world of reality. Everything we see and hear and touch may be as tricky an illusion as the reflection in a mirror or the mirage in a desert. What I believe Eddington called a dance of electrons. Curious, isn't it, that the Hindus called material life *maya*, or illusion, and their symbol for *maya* was *The Dancer*. In their mythology, her dance is supposed to distract man from contemplation of the reality beyond matter, the way an erotic dancer distracts his senses from other things – by the hypnotic effect of a rhythmically moving pattern.

'What is behind a *maya*'s dance? We don't know. Even our brains are a part of it and nothing more. How does your mind act on your body when you decide to move your arm? Neither psychology nor physiology can tell you . . . So they deny the duality of mind and body. Throughout the history of science, there has always been a tendency to deny whatever could not be explained, instead of saying simply: *We don't know*. The legend of the *doppelgänger* is very old. There is a word for it in all languages and . . .

'That, Dr Willing, is my third possibility: Suppose such things can happen? Suppose Faustina Crayle is abnormal in an extraordinary way that modern psychology will not acknowledge, let alone investigate?'

If Mrs Lightfoot feared an outbreak of that outraged incredulity that is a sure sign of basic credulity – the fool's fear of being fooled – she had misjudged her man. Basil spoke quietly: 'In other words, you're suggesting that Miss Crayle may be an unconscious medium?'

She flushed. 'I hate that word medium. I'm not just another sentimental egoist, longing for personal survival after death.'

'No, I shouldn't call you sentimental.' Basil's glance strayed to the lawn outside the window where the autumn breeze tumbled the dead leaves and pounced on them in erratic starts and sallies like an invisible kitten.

'But you would call me an egoist?'

'Perhaps.' He turned to face her. 'Confronted with an experience that shattered all your preconceptions of the universe, you did not investigate it. You were concerned only with its effect on your school. Why didn't you confront Miss Crayle herself with this? Give her a chance to make some explanation?'

'Really, Dr Willing. How could you or I or anyone suggest to any human being that she might be something monstrous beyond the pale of all known scientific fact and theory? If there are such things – have you ever thought how horrible it would be from the medium's own point of view? The almost universal assumption that you must be a fraud and the consequent loss of your normal social and economic life; the angry incredulity of science, the fanatic persecution of religion, the ridicule of the witty, the commercial exploitation of the cynical, and the fatuous faith of the superstitious, your only friend. And then – as if all that were not enough – you would have to face your own private, unprovable knowledge that you were the involuntary prey of forces unknown and abnormal, perhaps dangerous and evil. Forces that no one else in the whole world could help you to cope with. Could anyone be more utterly cut off from the rest of the human race? What a life of loneliness and terror! I should take to drink or drugs myself – as so many so-called mediums do . . . That is one reason I hope you are not going to repeat all this to Miss Crayle.'

'I still think she has a right to know the truth.'

'And I thought that, if I told you the truth, you would agree with me that she should not know it!'

Basil smiled. 'Your error.' He had risen, picking up hat and driving gloves. Suddenly he paused. 'How do you explain the fact that this double of Miss Crayle appeared only when she came to Brereton?'

Mrs Lightfoot had reserved her heavy ammunition for the last shot. 'I hadn't meant to tell you. Mollie Maidstone is a friend of mine. I got the truth out of her a few days ago, under pledge of secrecy, but – I'm going to tell you.'

'Tell me what?'

'That Miss Crayle left the Maidstone School last year under precisely the same conditions that she is now leaving Brereton.'

CHAPTER EIGHT

A star upon your birthday burned,
Whose fierce serene
Red pulseless planet never yearned
In Heaven, Faustine.

Gisela had wakened at dawn that same Thursday morning. Sunshine was pouring through her east window. She went downstairs to the front door. The world looked newly made in the clean light of the fledgeling sun. She had it all to herself. Even the maids had not come down yet.

She crossed the south lawn to an open vine-covered summer-house, placed there for its view of the cutting garden. It was an oblong, sunken garden, reached by a flight of stone steps. She went down the steps and along the path to the reflecting pool at the centre. In spring and early autumn, the spot was all syrupy scents and lush colours. Now there were only a few rusty, ragged chrysanthe-mums, distilling a fragrance more like spice than honey. She sat on a marble bench, resting her chin on her hand, looking at the placid surface of the pool.

'The early bird in luck again!'

She started at the sound of that young male voice. She looked up and saw a face that matched the voice – a classic oval that suggested Italian blood, yet the skin was English, fair and fine-textured as an infant's. Bright mischief in the blue eyes was softened by thick, golden lashes. The lip line was a subtle curve that seemed to quiver on the edge of mockery.

'I don't believe I know you.'

'But I know you.' Uninvited, he lounged at the other end of the bench, crossing long slim legs. 'You are Gisela von Hohenems. I've heard all about you from an unimpeachable source and I admire you tremendously.'

'Why?'

'Oh . . .' He made a large gesture. 'Penniless refugee, beautiful and young, making her way, like Ruth, through the alien corn. Even people who have never seen you must admire you and now I've seen you . . .' He smiled impudently.

'Sorry to spoil the romantic picture,' said Gisela. 'But I'm not very young and not at all penniless. I earn a good salary here.'

'The catch is in that word "earn". You shouldn't have to earn anything. You should simply sit still and look beautiful.'

'And be bored to death? No, thank you. Do you realize that you're in the grounds of a girls' school? We have fixed hours for male visitors. Six a. m. is not one of them.'

'More regimentation!' he exclaimed indignantly. 'I always break rules. Make a point of it.'

'I doubt if that explanation would satisfy our headmistress, Mrs Lightfoot.' Gisela rose. 'You can hardly be drunk, but . . .'

'Why not?'

'So early in the morning?'

'Another rule I make a point of breaking. But I'm not drunk this time. Merely – devastated. By you.'

'In other words, a cub-wolf intoxicated by his own technique.'

'Oh, Ray, darling, I didn't know you were here!' A small figure in dark-blue serge tumbled through the leafless honeysuckle, fair curls streaming behind her. 'Oh, Ray!' Margaret Vining catapulted into his arms and clung to him ecstatically.

'Hi, kid.' He disengaged himself gently and set the small girl down on her feet.

'Now I understand,' said Gisela. 'You're Margaret's brother, Raymond. And she is the unimpeachable source.'

'Right.' His smile faded as he looked down at the little girl clinging to his hand. He looked up at Gisela again, eyes sobered, almost penitent – only his lips still seemed to quiver on the edge of unborn laughter. The resemblance to Margaret was striking when they were together.

'Miss von Hohenems!' Margaret was still clinging to her brother's hand, looking up at him with adoring eyes. 'Do you think Mrs Lightfoot will let Ray take me out for breakfast at the village inn? He promised I could breakfast with him when he came here for the school party this afternoon. He said we could have griddle cakes and sausages and strawberry jam.'

'Not a vitamin in a carload,' added Vining, with a grin. 'From what I hear, the girls at Brereton are pretty sick of vitamins.'

'You may ask Mrs Lightfoot when she comes downstairs at eight o'clock,' Gisela told Vining.

'I'm sure she'll let me if Ray asks her.' Meg hopped on one foot, holding her brother's hand for balance. 'Ray always gets his own way with everybody.'

The 'school party' was a monthly event. After each meeting of the Board of Trustees, Mrs Lightfoot entertained them at tea with her teachers and pupils, who were encouraged to invite parents and other relatives. It was always an ordeal for the younger teachers to achieve the difficult blend of sophisticated elegance and pedagogic decorum which Mrs Lightfoot expected of them on these occasions.

That afternoon Gisela looked in her mirror and decided she had reached a happy compromise this time in a white wool dress with gold necklace and bracelets. As she went down the hall, the door of Alice Aitchison's room was standing wide open and Gisela saw in one glance that Alice had been less discreet.

She stood, profile to the open door, facing a dressing-table. She wore a long-skirted housecoat of corded silk the same vivid burnt orange as her scarf. There were outrageously high-heeled black suede pumps on her feet, with huge rhinestone buckles. The sleeves were elbow length, but the neckline dropped dangerously over her thrusting bosom. For the first time Gisela thought Alice beautiful, in a bold, hot-blooded way. But nothing could have been more inappropriate.

Alice turned and saw Gisela.

'You look the way Meg Vining or Beth Chase would look if they could dress as they pleased,' said Gisela.

'I don't care!' Alice surged forward in a magnificent swishing of silk. There was a high apricot colour in her cheeks. Her hazel eyes looked almost golden under the nut-brown hair.

'Have you considered Mrs Lightfoot's reaction?'

'Why should I? I shan't be here much longer!' She slipped an arm through Gisela's. 'Our dresses go well together. White and orange and we're both dark.'

'You're leaving?'

'I hope so.' She squeezed Gisela's arm. 'Today, I'm going to find out.'

'And if you don't?'

'Then nothing matters.'

No one noticed Gisela as the two women came through the archway into the big drawing-room. Alice paused on the threshold dramatically. Old Miss Chellis, in dingy blue taffeta, nearly dropped a teacup halfway to her lips. Mademoiselle de Vitré, in voluminous raisin velvet, looked envious and spiteful. Miss Dodd, the new art teacher from the Middle West, carefully smart in well-cut crêpe, looked as if she felt considerably less smart than she had intended to feel this afternoon. Silver-haired Mrs Greer, in pale blue with Parma violets, continued to look serene as always. But all the girls in white voile looked as if they were thinking: That's it! That's the way I'm going to dress the very first chance I get!

Gisela recalled that Alice herself was only a year or so older than the elder girls at Brereton.

Mrs Lightfoot herself was superb. Not by the quiver of an eyelash did she appear to notice the gaudy figure on the threshold. She went on talking to the elderly man at her elbow in a low, conversational tone, lips smiling, eyes indifferent.

Gisela was glad to find refuge with Mrs Chase, the mother of Elizabeth.

'I hear my little girl is going to be in the Greek play this year. To think of Elizabeth being able to speak Greek as well as read it! Those letters look just like chicken tracks to me! But, when I was a girl, women weren't supposed to learn things. Just a little French and dancing. I left school at sixteen, came out at seventeen, and married at eighteen. My first marriage, I mean.'

Gisela looked at Mrs Chase and wondered how old she really was. The reddish brown of her hair was as patently an artifice as the tomato-red of her lips and nails, and the harsh dyes only made her skin and eyes look more faded than ever. Her tilted nose and round chin were perennially childlike, but fine threads of scar at neck and hairline explained the synthetic smoothness of her cheeks. As she played with her gloves, two square emeralds flashed on her small, gnarled hands. The hands were ten years older than the face and the voice was ten years older than the hands.

'What's this play about?' went on Mrs Chase.

'*Medea*?' Gisela hesitated. 'It's a play about jealousy and murder.'

'Murder!' The emeralds were suddenly still. 'For a girls' school? Really, *Fräulein* . . .' Every German teacher was a 'Fräulein' to Mrs Chase as every French teacher was a 'Mademoiselle'.

'They all listen to "Gangbusters" on the radio,' returned Gisela. 'This is tragic poetry in the purest Greek tradition.'

'What part does Elizabeth play?'

'She and her friend Margaret Vining are playing Medea's sons, whom she murders to punish their father for infidelity.'

'A mother murdering her own children! And for such a reason! Girls shouldn't know about such things!'

'Isn't that just another way of saying that girls should not be educated at all?'

'Oh . . .'

At first Gisela thought Mrs Chase was still disconcerted by Euripides. Then she saw that Mrs Chase was no longer listening. She was looking toward the other end of the room, eyes blank with astonishment.

Alice Aitchison stood before an open french window, a splash of brilliance, drawing all glances in her direction as automatically as the calculated flash of colour in a roadside poster. Smoke trailed from a cigarette in one hand as she shook hot ashes dangerously near dry twigs of shrubbery outside. A man stood beside her, listening to whatever she was saying with a rather fatuous smile. He was in his forties, bald and fleshy. His aggressively rustic tweeds marked a city man spending an unaccustomed day in the country. In some indefinable way the tweeds and the thick-soled, highly polished walking shoes reeked of money.

'Who is that?' murmured Mrs Chase.

'The man or the girl?' asked Gisela.

'The girl.'

'Her name is Alice Aitchison. She is our dramatic coach. I don't know who the man is. Some relative perhaps.'

'What sort of girl is she?' Mrs Chase's gaze was still fixed on Alice.

'That's hard to say,' answered Gisela, cautiously. 'She gets on well with her pupils. She's a good coach.'

'I see.' Mrs Chase's mouth lost its immature pout, settled into an older, harder line. 'It's been so nice seeing you, Fräulein.' She smiled absently and started moving away through the crowd.

Gisela went on toward the tea-table. Another voice spoke close beside her. 'Is this how you earn that good salary? Boosting the values of classical education to nitwits like Dorothea Chase?'

She turned her head to meet Raymond Vining's amused eyes. 'You heard us?'

'I wouldn't have missed it for anything! Now she's always going to think Euripides was the Edgar Wallace of his day!'

'Oh, dear! I hope she won't ask Mrs Lightfoot to replace *Medea* with *Pollyanna* or *Daddy Long Legs*.'

'I'm sure that's just what she's doing now.'

Gisela's glance followed his to the table where Mrs Chase had just accosted Mrs Lightfoot. They were standing within a few feet of the open window where Alice Aitchison was still talking to the man in tweeds. Some impulse prompted Gisela to ask: 'Do you know who that man is?'

'Alice's fat friend? Floyd Chase, the stockbroker. Beth's father. Dorothea's former husband. I'm sure Dorothea wouldn't have come here today if she'd known he was coming too. But, after all, he is the child's father. I always feel sorry for a childlike Beth, shuttled back and forth between warring parents.'

'Wouldn't it be worse to live in the same house with warring parents all the time?' returned Gisela.

'Of course.'

Vining's smile mocked her and himself and the world all at once.

'But you mustn't say so. We've got to have some apparently rational justification for marriage now that the mystical justification is no longer valid. So we pretend that quarrelling within the marriage bond is salutary for children while ending the quarrel by ending the marriage will wreck their mental health for ever after. And just think what a comfort that idea must be to people who can't afford divorce. Instead of merely feeling poor, they can feel morally superior.'

'You're a misanthropist!'

'Alice must have been telling you about me!'

'You mean Alice Aitchison? You know her?'

'Pretty well. We used to be engaged once upon a time.' He

glanced across the room toward the orange dress and a daredevil spark came into his eyes. 'Alice likes money. Floyd Chase has plenty of it. I haven't.'

'You're frank.'

'Oh, it pays to tell the truth, because no one ever believes you. Everyone assumes you're hiding or distorting something and looks for the real truth elsewhere. I don't like tea-parties. I'm going down the drive to the place where I left my car. There's a fifth of Bourbon in the glove compartment. Would you care to come along?'

'No, thank you!' Gisela was amused at his unquenchable impudence. 'I like tea and . . .'

Before Gisela could go on, Arlene appeared at her elbow.

'Excuse me, Miss von Hohenems, but you're wanted on the telephone – long distance.'

'Thank you. Who is it?'

A sly curiosity peeked through the mask of the trained servant. 'Miss Crayle.'

Gisela hurried toward the door. As she passed the window, where Alice and Chase were standing, Alice called out: 'Gisela! Do you know Mr Chase? Miss von Hohenems.'

Gisela apologized. 'I must run. I'm on my way to the telephone.'

Alice was amused. 'Your psychiatrist friend is running up quite a telephone bill.'

'This time it's Faustina.'

'Is that wretched fool still pestering you?'

Gisela was glad to get away to the telephone booth under the stairs.

'Hello!'

A small, faraway voice answered: 'Gisela? This is Faustina.'

'How are you? I hope you're having a good rest.'

I'm all right.' The words came slowly, languidly, as if it were a great effort to force them out one by one. 'But I miss you. Have you any news for me?'

'News?'

'Didn't Dr Willing see Mrs Lightfoot? He said he was going to.'

'Oh. yes. He was here this morning. I couldn't see him then. I had a class.'

'What did she say?'

'I don't know, but I'm sure he'll let you know as soon as he can. Probably this evening.'

'I hope so. I get so anxious just waiting.'

'How much longer are you going to be in town?'

'Until Friday. Then I'm going down to Brightsea in New Jersey. I have a cottage there. Could you come down for the week-end?'

'I'd love to, only – I have a dinner engagement Friday evening,' said Gisela. 'Why don't you stay in New York another day so I can see you there?'

'I'm going to meet someone else at the cottage Friday evening. Someone I'd like you to meet, too. Could you come late in the evening, after dinner?"

'I don't know if I can. May I call you tomorrow? At what time?'

'Don't bother to call me. Just come any time you can Friday or Saturday or Sunday. I haven't any engagements of my own except this one Friday evening.' The voice was tepid and slower than ever – almost lethargic.

'Then make some!' returned Gisela, briskly. 'Have a real holiday while you're still in New York. You need it. Look up your old friends.'

'I haven't any.'

'Then go to a play. Do some shopping. Buy something you can't afford. Preferably a hat you don't need. Will you?'

'I'll try to. Good-bye, Gisela.'

'Good-bye.'

She put the telephone down with a sense of guilt. Out of sight, out of mind. In the last few hours she had not thought of Faustina. Already the forlorn little figure was diminishing, receding toward the horizon of memory. Mrs Lightfoot was right: with Faustina gone the whole queer business would be forgotten in a month or so by everyone at Brereton. One of the many small things, unexplained and unexplainable, that we all put aside in the course of a busy lifetime. Years from now, some woman might say to a group of friends, sitting around a campfire on Hallowe'en: 'Nothing queer ever happened to me – except one rather odd thing when I was a girl at school. No, it was never explained. There was a young art teacher and she . . .' The rest would be a cloudy memory, distorted by all the other more personal memories of the years between . . .

Gisela returned to the drawing-room for a cup of tea and took it over to the window where Alice had been standing with Chase. There was no sign of Alice now. Chase and Vining had disappeared also. Gisela wondered if all three had gone down to Vining's car for a sip of something stronger than tea. That would be just like Alice . . .

As Gisela lifted her teacup she glanced through the window across the garden to the open summerhouse that looked so raw and unsheltered in the leafless November landscape. She thought she saw something moving in the dim interior, but she couldn't be sure at such a distance – at least five hundred feet. A flash of burnt orange drew her eyes down to the cutting garden below the summerhouse. She put down her teacup and stepped through the window. A few moments later she was running down the stone steps.

Alice Aitchison lay on the ground in the bright, cold sunlight. Her head rested on the bottom step. Her painted lips were red as fresh blood against the ghastly pallor of her face. Even before Gisela leaned over to touch the still hand, she knew that Alice was dead.

She straightened, almost overcome by sudden, giddy nausea. She was quite alone with the dead woman in the windy sunlight. As the whole school had been studying Euripides, his words came back to her: 'What deed of horror may we not expect from that high-soaring, unrepentant spirit, spurred by despair?'

Alice was a Medea – high-spirited, unrepenting. This afternoon she had spoken of leaving Brereton like a woman goaded by despair: *Then nothing matters* . . . But it could be called an accident, Gisela told herself fiercely. And it should be. No one need ever know that it was suicide. It would have been so easy for one of those high heels to catch in the hem of that long trailing skirt. There was even a slight rip in the hem to make the idea seem plausible. And one of the shoes had come off. It was lying upturned at a little distance from the body . . .

She ran up the steps. More slowly she crossed the lawn to the drawing-room window. She picked her way through the crowd, trying to make herself as inconspicuous as possible until she came to Mrs Lightfoot. Before Gisela could utter a word, Mrs Lightfoot spoke almost inaudibly.

'Where have you been? It is hardly civil to our guests. I don't see Miss Aitchison either. Do you know where she is?'

'I'm sorry.' Gisela's voice was pitched equally low. 'I was called to the telephone. When I came back, I happened to look toward the cutting garden. Alice Aitchison is lying at the foot of the steps and – she's dead.'

Never had Gisela admired Mrs Lightfoot more than at that moment. Her lips barely moved. 'Are you sure?'

'Yes. I touched her.'

'Show me.' Mrs Lightfoot rose without any suggestion of haste. There was a slight smile of apology on her lips as she made her way through the crowd. Everyone must have thought she was being called away on the most trivial errand. But once outside, her smile vanished and she walked swiftly. When they reached the foot of the steps she did not kneel to touch Alice as Gisela had done. She stood still, looking down at the dead girl with an inscrutable expression. Finally it was Gisela who said:

'Shouldn't I get a doctor? There are cases of catalepsy that look like death . . .'

'I know death when I see it,' answered Mrs Lightfoot. 'Look at her neck. It's broken. You know what this means. An inquest. And I don't even know whether there's a coroner or a medical examiner in Connecticut.'

'I thought we could call it an accident,' said Gisela.

Mrs Lightfoot started and looked at her with sudden intensity. 'What else could it be?'

'Well,' Gisela hesitated. 'There's always the possibility of suicide . . .'

'Nonsense.' Mrs Lightfoot was emphatic. 'We'll have no scandal here, if you please. I suppose there'll have to be an inquest, but the verdict is a foregone conclusion – accident. Look at that torn hem and the high-heeled shoe that's fallen off. That's how she tripped. There's no man here I can trust except Spencer, my chauffeur. Go up to the garage and tell him to come down here without speaking to anyone else about it. If he can get the body up to the garage before the party is over, no one else need know about this until we call the police. I don't want these young girls or their parents to have the shock of seeing her.'

'But you can't move the body!' exclaimed Gisela. 'Not until the police have seen it.'

'Surely in these circumstances . . .'

'Can I be of any assistance?'

The cheerful male voice came from the head of the steps. Both women looked up. Floyd Chase was standing there smiling inanely. It seemed to Gisela that Mrs Lightfoot grew visibly older in that moment. 'Too late now,' she muttered.

Chase was coming down the steps. 'Has someone fainted?' He was still smiling. 'Why, it's Alice!' He stopped as he neared the last step. 'My God!'

'Mr Chase, there has been an accident,' said Mrs Lightfoot. 'And you can help us – if you will stand at the head of the steps and keep anyone else from coming down until the body has been removed. I'm sure you'll understand that we don't want any of the pupils to see a thing like this.'

He looked at Mrs Lightfoot as if he had not heard a word she said. 'How did it happen?' he demanded hoarsely.

'I don't know,' retorted Mrs Lightfoot impatiently. 'The last time I saw Miss Aitchison she was in the drawing-room talking to you.'

'We were interrupted by my former wife.' He spoke in a dazed voice. 'Alice left us at once. By way of the french window. I had a few words with Dorothea. But I got away from her as soon as I could and came outdoors to look for Alice . . .'

'And where did your wife go?'

'I don't know.'

'Floyd!' On cue came the discontented whimper of Dorothea Chase. 'What are you doing down there? I've been looking for you everywhere – even in the kitchen garden!' She already had one foot on the top step. Beth, a small figure in white, was tugging at her mother's hand, trying to pull her down the steps.

'There she is, mother!' cried Beth. 'I didn't imagine anything. It really happened!'

'Dorothea!' Chase started up the steps. 'Don't bring the child down here. Please!'

For the first time Gisela felt some sympathy for the man as his wife answered shrewishly: 'She's bringing me – I'm not bringing her! And I shall certainly come down now to find out why you don't want me to! I . . .'

Her voice failed and she stood still, looking down incredulously at the broken body of the dead woman.

'Elizabeth!' she exclaimed. 'Go back upstairs at once!'

But Beth Chase stood beside her mother without moving. She, too, was looking down at the body with a mixture of horror and interest.

Chase swore under his breath. Mrs Lightfoot took a step forward, interposing her full skirt between the child and her view of Alice.

'Mrs Chase, did you happen to see Miss Aitchison here while you were outdoors, looking for your husband?'

'No, I was on the other side of the house.' Mrs Chase answered indifferently, as if she were too dense to catch the import of the question.

'But I saw her!'

Everyone turned to look at Beth. She seemed unable to realize the effect of the words she had just spoken in her thin, high voice. 'Mother asked me to find father. I came around on this side of the house by myself. I looked down the garden toward the summer-house. Miss Aitchison was standing at the head of the steps.'

"What was she doing?' asked Chase.

'Talking.'

'Then . . .' Mrs Lightfoot forced out the words. 'She was not alone?'

'Oh, no, Mrs Lightfoot. I didn't say she was alone, did I?'

'Who was with her?' insisted Chase hoarsely.

'Another teacher. The pale, thin one who used to teach drawing, Miss Crayle.'

'That's impossible!' cried Gisela. 'She just called me long distance from New York!'

'But I saw her, Miss von Hohenems,' protested Beth. 'When I told mother she wouldn't believe me either, so I brought her here to see for herself. Miss Crayle was wearing the blue coat and brown hat just as she always did. When Miss Aitchison came around the corner of the summerhouse, Miss Crayle was standing there, waiting. Miss Aitchison said something I didn't hear. Then Miss Crayle put out her hand and pushed Miss Aitchison and she screamed and fell backwards – down the steps. Then Miss Crayle went away as she always did – quite quietly, without making a sound . . .'

CHAPTER NINE

He who cast seven devils out
Of Magdalene
Could hardly do as much, I doubt,
For you, Faustine.

That night officers and trustees of the Murray Hill Hospital held a meeting in the office of the chairman, a newspaper publisher. It was after midnight when Basil came out of the building and walked up Broadway toward the Seventh Avenue parking lot where he had left his car.

Peace had made Broadway once more as tawdry as Coney Island. Tired as he was, huge signs of moving neon or electric light forced his attention on this company's cigarette and that company's whisky. They were the negation of art – giant, mechanical toys made for overgrown children who delighted in obvious catchwords, primary colours, and simple, repetitive motions.

The combined light of all these signs bathed the grimy asphalt underfoot in a false daylight. When a newsboy thrust a copy of tomorrow morning's paper into his hand, it was by this sick, unnatural light that he saw the headline on the first page: NECK BROKEN, TEACHER DIES. It was the dateline that held his attention: *Brereton, Thursday, 17 November* . . . He halted where he was to read the rest.

Miss Alice Aitchison, dramatic coach at the Brereton school for girls near here, was found dead in the school grounds at five o'clock this afternoon by another teacher, Miss Grizel von Hohenstein. The body was lying at the foot of some stone steps leading to a flower garden. According to the police, Miss Aitchison died of a broken neck sustained when she fell down the steps after catching a three-inch heel in the torn hem of an ankle-length housecoat of pale-blue taffeta which she was wearing at the time.

The accident was said to have been witnessed by one of the pupils, Miss Elizabeth Chase, aged thirteen, who ran to inform her mother, then visiting the school, just before Miss von Hohenstein discovered the body independently. Floyd Chase, the child's father, refused to let reporters interview her, but it is rumoured that she saw Miss Aitchison talking to a former teacher of the school, Miss Faustina Crayle, just before the tragedy. Miss Crayle, now staying at a midtown hotel in Manhattan, could not be reached for questioning at a late hour this evening.

Miss Aitchison was a daughter of the late Stanley Mordaunt Aitchison, investment banker, who committed suicide in 1945, after suffering financial reverses in Wall Street. The funeral will be private.

Basil thrust the folded paper into his overcoat pocket and hurried on to his car. If 'Grizel von Hohenstein' was as near as the reporter could get to Gisela's name, his story could not be trusted in other details and yet . . . Basil twirled the steering-wheel and the car swung into the stream of uptown traffic.

It was one a.m. when he reached the Fontainebleau, and the

lobby was empty. He gave his card to the night clerk. 'I'm not a reporter and I must see Miss Crayle at once. Will you tell her that I'm downstairs?'

'Her phone's been shut off since six p.m.,' answered the clerk. 'She's probably asleep now and . . .'

'This is urgent.'

The clerk looked at the card again, then turned to the house telephone. 'Miss Crayle will be down in a few moments.'

As she crossed the lobby, Basil had his first steady look at her in a clear light. She still seemed greyhound-thin and fragile, but she was no longer romantically ethereal – merely emaciated and bloodless. Her light-tan hair was thin and dry; her milky-blue eyes dreamy, abstracted. She wore a knitted dress of limp brown wool and her sallow skin was marred by a tiny red pimple on one cheek. All that remained of her wraithlike charm in the half-light was her quietness and gentleness.

They found chairs in a corner of the lobby. Basil offered cigarettes, but she declined. 'You saw her? Mrs Lightfoot?'

'Yes.' Basil lit a cigarette for himself and leaned back in his chair. 'Miss Crayle, where were you this afternoon at five o'clock?'

'Here, upstairs in my room.'

'Alone?'

'Yes.'

'What were you doing?'

'At five? I was talking to Gisela on the long-distance telephone. I've already explained that to a man from the New York Police Department. The Connecticut police sent him to question me this evening. Then reporters began calling me and I had my telephone shut off.'

'Do you know why the police questioned you?'

'Because of Alice Aitchison's death. They said it was just routine.'

'They always say it's "just routine". It never is.' Basil took the newspaper out of his pocket. 'Read this, please.'

She got as far as the second paragraph. Then the paper dropped from her hand. 'But that's impossible! I wasn't anywhere near Brereton this afternoon. My telephone call to Gisela proves it.'

'That's probably why you were not questioned any further.'

'Fortunately I can prove that I was here all day. There's only this one entrance at the Fontainebleau. The elevator men, the room clerks, the doormen all know me by sight. They know I didn't go out all afternoon or evening.'

'What about fire stairs? Or service entrance?'

'The police checked all that. You can only reach the service entrance by going through the restaurant kitchen. A cook and two helpers were there all afternoon. And the fire stairs open into the kitchen corridor. No one could have gone through without being seen and heard.'

'What did you do after your telephone conversation with Gisela?'

'After . . . ? Why I – I went to sleep.'

'At five in the afternoon?'

'Yes. I felt sleepy while I was talking to Gisela. Since I came here, I've fallen into the habit of sleeping a little in the afternoon especially when I've had tea.'

Basil nodded, understanding the things she had not said. She was so stunned by her dismissal from Brereton – so listless and defeated and bored – that she sought escape from reality in daytime sleep, like an old woman or a baby, unable to sustain the burden of consciousness for any length of time.

The chill he felt did not come entirely from the raw November night. *A sleepwalker will carry out in his sleep an impulse which he has previously suppressed in his waking state . . .*

'Did you ever have any impulse to kill Alice Aitchison?'

'Oh, no!' She seemed sincerely shocked. But such an impulse would have to be suppressed, unconscious. She would not know anything about it.

'You didn't like her, did you?'

'No,' admitted Faustina. 'I can't say I liked her. She was crude and she was always rather unkind to me. Sometimes I hated her . . .'

Again Basil nodded. He could see Faustina hating Alice – the weak hating the strong, calling her own weakness 'refinement' and the other's strength 'crudeness'. Those who cannot strike their enemies in the flesh strike at phantoms of their enemies in the safety and freedom of their own minds. To hate anyone is to wish for his obliteration and there is only one way to obliterate a human being – by death. Children know this instinctively when they shout: *I hate you! I wish you were dead!* Had Faustina lain down this afternoon with a sadistic fantasy of Alice's death in her mind? Had she slipped into sleep with that death-wish her last waking thought? Had she then risen in a sleepwalker's trance and . . . ?

No. The time element made it impossible. Asleep or awake, Faustina could not leave the Fontainebleau unseen, could not get to Connecticut from New York in the few minutes that intervened between her telephone call to Gisela and Alice Aitchison's death. Unless . . . *an unconscious mind could gather unto itself enough vital energy to project some purely visual image or reflection of itself on the air . . . rainbows and mirages do not exist in normal terms of space-time . . .*

Death by wishing – the crime attributed to witches from time immemorial. He smiled at the quaint, archaic idea, yet atavism gave it a curiously strong pull at the soft underside of the mind, like a rip tide . . .

'No doubt the Connecticut police decided that Elizabeth Chase was mistaken or hysterical. After all, she's only thirteen. But – she saw something, Miss Crayle. What was it?'

'I – I don't know.'

'I think you do know – or suspect.'

The blue eyes blurred as they slipped out of focus. She sat still and lifeless, as if she had withdrawn from the surface of her body into some dream of her own, more comforting than reality.

What had Black Andie's father said of Tod Lapraik? *I think folk have burned for dreams like yon* . . . In the broad Scots, it was more impressive: *I think folk hae brunt far dwams like yon* . . . And it was true. In other times, hundreds of Faustina Crayles had charred alive, writhing and shrieking, a human sacrifice to the gods of ignorance and terror . . .

'Come, Miss Crayle! You're not playing fair with me. Yesterday you knew what Mrs Lightfoot was going to tell me. Let's begin at the beginning. Why did you leave the Maidstone School last year?'

She started and winced. As if it were painful to return to the surface of her body and communicate with the world outside herself. Still she was silent. She would not give him a lead.

'Are you asking me to believe that you do not know the old

English tradition of the *fetch* – the phantom double of a living man? The same thing as the German *doppelgänger*, literally, the double-goer? If that were so, you would not have borrowed Gisela's copy of Goethe.'

He had anticipated various responses – surprise, indignation, denial. It had not occurred to him that she would cover her face with her hands and burst into tears. 'Dr Willing! What am I going to do?'

He glanced across the lobby to the desk. The clerk was a good forty feet away, his eyes bent on a ledger and, even in despair, Faustina wept quietly. He had not noticed her or anything else in the shadowy corner where they were sitting.

'Why didn't you tell me before you sent me to Mrs Lightfoot?'

'I didn't send you!' She protested weakly. 'It was you who insisted on going. And I – I don't *know* anything.' Her hands dropped. She turned her face toward him in an agony of distress, unconscious of reddened eyelids and stained cheeks. 'I've never seen – it. I don't know what – it is. I know only what people told me at Maidstone. Now – I suppose it's happened again at Brereton. But I didn't know. Mrs Lightfoot wouldn't tell me. I couldn't ask her. I did think she might tell you. That's why I let you go. And I couldn't tell you a thing like that before you went. You would have laughed. Or you would have thought me neurotic. A year ago I would have thought anyone insane who took such a thing seriously. But I knew that if you heard it from Mrs Lightfoot, you wouldn't laugh. You'd listen to her, even if you didn't believe what she said. At the worst you'd think she was the neurotic instead of me.'

'Do you think Mrs Lightfoot is neurotic?'

'Was Miss Maidstone neurotic? And all the other teachers

and pupils and servants in both schools? Dr Willing, when you've lost your job twice because of a thing, you don't laugh and say it's all imagination. I don't know what this thing is. It may not be what they say it is. But it isn't imaginary. There's something – I mean, something real. And it isn't me myself. I know I'm not a fraud. You don't know that, of course. You can't, because you have only my word for it. But I do know it. What remains? That I do these things unconsciously? That's physically impossible. Even in a sleepwalking state, I could not be in two places at the same time and that's what they tell me has happened – more than once. Are they all conspiring to play an elaborate hoax on me? I cannot see people as dissimilar as Miss Maidstone in Virginia and Arlene Murphy in Connecticut involved in the same pointless conspiracy, solemnly acting out a futile farce over a period of twelve months just to discomfit me. So now what remains? I don't know, but – I'm afraid.'

She looked beyond him, into the brightly lighted vacancy of the lobby. 'Have you any idea what all this is like for me? How desperately I keep asking myself all the old unanswered questions: What is life for? Why were human beings made? Why do we assume so confidently that God is good, when He is so much more likely to be evil? Are we an accident of chemistry, without beginning or end or purpose? Super-colloids, acting out a heartless comedy? Are we a dream of God's, as the Buddhists believe? Is that why, in early childhood, you stare at your face in the mirror and look at your hands and feet and say to yourself: *I am me. I am Faustina Crayle. I am not anyone else.* Yet, no matter how hard you try to realize your identity something inside you goes on feeling that it's not quite true. That you are only Faustina Crayle temporarily and locally. That you could so easily be someone else. That's what makes life so dreamlike – your own sense of your own unreality . . .

'I've read all the standard books on philosophy, science, and religion. They have nothing to do with the urgency of real life and personal problems. Do these men, playing a sort of intellectual chess with themselves, have any idea how ordinary people in trouble long for an answer that satisfies both heart and reason? You ask for bread and they give you – words. How can I live with a thing like this all the rest of my life? What is going to become of me?' Again she began to weep softly. Basil waited until she had tired herself out. Then he said, patiently: 'Tell me what happened at Maidstone.'

He caught a hint of lavender as she took out a handkerchief to mop her eyes. Her face smoothed itself into some semblance of composure, but her voice was still throaty, vibrant. 'That was my first job after I left college. I was happy and proud when I went to Maidstone. It's a boarding school, rather like Brereton, only it's larger and in Virginia instead of Connecticut and the girls don't wear uniforms. It's more athletic. The girls all hike and ride and swim. But it's just as strict as Brereton, even stricter. No male visitors, except Sunday afternoons, and that sort of thing.

'After I'd been there a week, I began to have a feeling that I was being watched and talked about. Why, I didn't know. I would feel that one of the girls was looking at me curiously and when I turned to look at her, she would look away. When I entered a room where people were talking, everyone would stop and then go on in a different tone of voice. So I would know they'd been talking about me. But I had no idea what they'd been saying. The other teachers seemed to avoid me. The girls were uneasy and reserved with me. The servants seemed to fear and hate me, just as they did at Brereton afterward. But this was the first time anything of the sort had happened to me, so I didn't take it too seriously. I thought they just didn't like me or something about me – my clothes, or speech, or manner.

'Gradually a pattern began to emerge. I would meet someone on the stairs or in the hall. That person would look surprised or puzzled and say: "How did you get here? I just saw you upstairs." And I'd answer ingenuously: "You must be mistaken. I've been in the garden all afternoon." Or the library, or wherever I had been. Then the look of surprise would give way to suspicion. After that had happened two or three times, I began to ask myself: *What is this? Why are people always thinking they see me in places where I can't possibly have been at the time?* I was as puzzled as anyone else. I didn't dare mention it to anyone. No one mentioned it to me. But it was so inexplicable that it worried me from the first. Eventually it began to frighten me. So I stopped telling people where I had been when they were surprised to find me where I was . . . Then came a note from Miss Maidstone herself – dismissal with a cheque for a year's services.

'I was braver then than I am now. And Miss Maidstone was a soft-spoken Virginian, more approachable than Mrs Lightfoot, who is all Yankee Puritan at heart. I took the note to Miss Maidstone's study. She was evasive at first, but my distress broke her resistance at last. She took some books from a locked cupboard and told me to read them.

'I sat up all that night, reading those books. I could hardly understand what they were about. I had always laughed at spiritualists and I knew they were equally despised by religion and science. But these men weren't spiritualists. They didn't believe in ghosts or personal immortality. Most of them were atheists. But they did believe that there was a small group of inexplicable phenomena that had been outlawed by orthodox science without examination. And they weren't obscure cranks. One was William James, the psychologist, who investigated such things privately because his career would have been jeopardized if he had done so publicly. Another was Charles Richet, the physiologist, who did it publicly and endured the bombardment of ridicule that followed as the tax a breaker of taboos must always pay to orthodoxy.

'I soon began to understand why Miss Maidstone had lent me these particular books. There were a few dry, unemotional, apparently factual accounts of so-called "doubles" – the dreams of the waking, the ghosts of the living. Goethe's experience was mentioned. That's why I borrowed Gisela's copy of his *Memoirs*. And there was one case of a young French teacher in Livonia nearly a hundred years ago that was extraordinarily like my own.

'It was at that point I pushed all the books aside and sat there, alone in my room at Maidstone, looking out of the window at Orion and the Big Dipper. Echoes of the last few weeks were resounding in my mind: Miss Crayle, what are you doing upstairs? A moment ago I looked out the window and saw you walking down the drive . . . "Miss Crayle, was that you on the balcony just now? I thought you were playing the piano in the music room" . . . Things that had happened not once but five or six times altogether.

'I didn't want to read any more, because the men who had collected and correlated those few cases made no attempt to explain the thing. They were all scientists, agnostics by temperament. They simply reported the words of eyewitnesses and said, in effect: These people say this happened. We grant it more than probable that they are all liars. But for the sake of argument let us suppose they are not liars. In that case – if they are telling the truth as they saw it – what caused this? How was it contrived and what does it mean?

"'If they are telling the truth" – that "if" haunted me. I didn't know the answer any more than they did. But at least I did know now what people were saying and thinking about me at Maidstone.

'I didn't quite believe in it myself then, but I was frightened because I knew there must be something back of all this . . . Perhaps only a silly trick or joke, but still – something inimical to me. And I did not know what it was.

'Next morning I went down to Miss Maidstone's study to return the books. She told me that she kept her interest in such matters secret because strict orthodoxy is exacted from a schoolmistress. She was kind. She talked quite seriously about my "psychic power". She really did believe in it. But, for that very reason, she would not keep me at Maidstone a moment longer. You see, Mrs Lightfoot got rid of me because she thought I was either a trickster or a victim of trickery, but Miss Maidstone dismissed me because she was so sure that I was not a trickster. That was far more disturbing to her. And to me. If she had accused me of trickery, I could have denied it and substantiated my denial. I had no defence against this other charge. I couldn't prove anything. I didn't know the truth myself.

'Miss Maidstone was very sorry for me because she did not believe that I was to blame in any way. In a moment of weakness, she wrote me the letter of recommendation that got me the job at Brereton afterward and . . .'

'Let me interrupt at this point,' said Basil. 'How often was the double seen at Maidstone?'

'I didn't keep count of the first few incidents because I attached no importance to them. Afterward, when I talked it over with Miss Maidstone, she said it had been seen seven times. Twice at night on the lawn from an upstairs window while I was asleep in my own room. Three times in the morning, on an upstairs balcony from the front drive while I was teaching in a classroom downstairs. Twice in the afternoon, passing outside an open window at the end of the front hall, while I was standing inside the front door.'

'Were you wearing the same brown hat and blue coat on these occasions?'

'The same hat, but not the same coat. I had a camel's-hair coat then. They were popular at Maidstone. Just right for the winter climate there.'

'And yet, after all this, you went on to Brereton?'

'At that stage, I think I was more puzzled than frightened. Even if the whole thing was not an elaborate hoax even – if the so-called "double" was some sort of collective hallucination – it had never happened to me before and I thought that something peculiar to Maidstone might have caused it – something in the climate or the psychological condition at the school that would not recur elsewhere.

'I knew that I was extraordinarily lucky to get the job at Brereton after leaving Maidstone so ignominiously. I tried desperately to please everyone there and during my first week I seemed to be succeeding. I remember that week as a relatively happy time, my first in the last year, and then . . . One day I met old Miss Chellis in the upstairs hall and she said: "Miss Crayle, Mrs Lightfoot doesn't care to have teachers use the back stairs." I said: "I beg your pardon, but I haven't been using the back stairs, Miss Chellis." She answered: "No? I saw you in the garden a moment ago. Now I come up the front stairs and find you here in the upper hall. You didn't pass me on the front stairs, so . . ."

'Then I knew. It was going to happen all over again. That was when I really began to be afraid. How could it have followed me all the way from Maidstone to Brereton nearly a year later unless it was real? I, myself, was the only connecting link between the two schools so I, myself, must be the cause. If it had been revealed to me as a trick then I should have hugged the trickster. It would have been such a relief . . .'

'There was at least one other connecting link between Maidstone and Brereton,' said Basil. 'Alice Aitchison. Have you any idea why she said Gisela would be sorry if she asked me to investigate the gossip about you?'

'I suppose Alice meant that Mrs Lightfoot would be angry at Gisela if she told an outsider what was going on in the school.'

'Was Miss Aitchison one of those who saw the double at Maidstone?'

'Oh, no, but she had heard all the stories about me there. Everyone at Maidstone had heard those stories. When I found Alice at Brereton this fall, I was dreadfully afraid she would repeat those Maidstone stories there. The first time we were alone together I begged her to promise she would not tell anyone at Brereton. She promised and I really think she kept her promise. But she used to say things to me about it before other people –

cryptic things that I could understand while the others couldn't. She knew that kept me on tenterhooks and she enjoyed seeing me squirm. The day I left she even said she had seen my face at an upper window when I was in the garden. But I knew she was only pretending she had seen it in order to worry me and startle one of the maids.'

'How could you know that?'

'Because she wasn't afraid. Her eyes mocked me when she said it. You see, Alice thought I was responsible for the whole thing. That day she promised she wouldn't tell anyone at Brereton tears came into my eyes and then she went on in that cruel voice of hers: "You shy, inhibited girls always develop hysteria. But if you want to keep your job here, you'll have to learn to govern your sub-conscious impulses."

'I was utterly taken aback. I questioned her and she told me that there was only one reasonable explanation – that I was the one who was playing tricks – that I did these things in some sort of sleepwalking state without remembering them afterward. Perhaps that is why Alice was always so contemptuous of me, never afraid of me the way the others were, and . . .' Faustina hesitated, went on more slowly, 'perhaps that's what killed her.'

Basil was startled. 'What do you mean?'

'Think, Dr Willing – how was Alice killed. Not by anything tangible – rope or knife or bullet. She tripped and fell down a flight of stone steps, breaking her neck. An accident. But don't so-called "accidents" come as often from within as from without? Haven't insurance companies compiled statistics to show that certain people are "accident prone"?'

'Yes,' he agreed. 'Big business has come to the rescue of Freud. He had a theory that accidents happen to people who have a guilty impulse to self-punishment. A high heel and a trailing skirt might be the occasion of an accident, but not its cause. That would lie deeper in the victim's own traitorous mind – a sort of unconscious suicide.'

'Well, suppose one person's subconscious mind had access to another person's subconscious and planted the suicidal impulse without either being aware of the process – that would be murder, wouldn't it? A new form of murder quite undetectable – unknown even to the murderer himself as well as his victim. Poets have been saying for centuries that all hate is murder. They may be right.'

'Murder by telepathy?' Basil smiled. 'Then none of us would be safe! Fortunately, as yet there is no real evidence that the mind of one person can influence the mind of another person at a distance without hypnosis.'

'I was not thinking of anything like telepathy or hypnosis,' responded Faustina. 'I was thinking . . .'

'Yes?' Basil encouraged her.

'I was thinking that little Beth Chase's testimony may be true. People trip and fall when they are startled. A cast shoe, a torn hem are as often the result of a fall as its cause. What would be certain to startle Alice Aitchison? A vision of me standing on the garden steps at Brereton when she knew that Gisela was talking to me on the long-distance telephone to New York.

'You see, Alice did know all the stories about me, and she had never believed them. For that very reason the shock would be all the greater if she suddenly came face to face with me at Brereton in broad daylight when she knew beyond a shadow of doubt that I was really in New York. It would be a peculiarly dreadful shock to find that the thing you had always laughed at was real. And if the thing put out a hand to touch you – surely you might be frightened enough to trip and fall down a flight of steps . . .'

'And you're beginning to think that Alice saw that vision of you because you hated Alice and sent the vision to her when you were asleep without knowing anything about it consciously?'

Faustina answered desperately: 'What other explanation covers all the facts?'

Basil studied Faustina's face. A faint flush of excitement gave it a new quality – the radiance that comes and goes so unexpectedly in the transparent skin of the very fair. If she had more vitality – a higher rate of metabolism – warmer, quicker blood – she might have been attractive, even beautiful. Bone structure and colouring were basically good. It was something sluggish and *piano* in her nature that made her so colourless and negligible most of the time. But now he had a glimpse of what she might have been.

He was sure that the despair she felt was sincere. But he was also sure that, paradoxically, this despair was now blended with pleasure in a certain sense of power, as agreeable as it was unaccustomed. She had not asked for power, but now she believed it had been thrust upon her, she would have been less than human if she had not felt something more complex than unmixed horror. The horror was there, but with it were other, more subtle feelings. She could not be wholly dismayed at the idea that she, Faustina Crayle, plain, timid, and neglected, had punished with death the bold, handsome woman who scoffed at all her failings with such arrogant cruelty.

For the first time Basil understood why so many seventeenth-century witches and warlocks had confessed to the crimes they were accused of with a wealth of gleeful detail. It was not torture alone that had wrung those false confessions from them. They had enjoyed terrifying their persecutors, even while they themselves were dying a horrible death. It was the only revenge open to them. No doubt the more deluded had even persuaded themselves that they had mysterious power, for that would be much more pleasant than seeing oneself as a helpless victim of barbarism. It was significant that witches had always been people without any wholesome outlet for the sense of power.

Mony a time I have askit mysel' why witches and warlocks should be auld, duddy, wrunkl't wives or auld, feckless, doddered men . . . Or, Black Andie might have added, forlorn young girls without looks or property or position in life. Psychologically, witches came from the same stratum as poisoners and hysterics – frustrated outcasts, taking a sly, perverse revenge on a society that gave them little opportunity for pleasure or pride.

But, granting all this, the great question remained unanswered: Was their revenge purely a matter of self-delusion? Or was a human creature, under extreme psychological stress, able, for that very reason, to exercise peculiar mental power unknown to healthy people, leading ordinary lives? Was it accident that all the religions of the world used the three great frustrations – celibacy, fasting, and poverty – as a recognized material mechanism for producing visions they regarded as spiritual?

'I don't believe you need shoulder the guilt for Miss Aitchison's death,' said Basil at last. 'In science there is a ratio between the proof required and the probability of the thing you are trying to prove. It takes relatively little evidence to establish something that fits comfortably into the pattern of other facts, already established. But when you are trying to prove something which is contrary to every accepted fact and theory – then, naturally, you need a mountain of irreproachable evidence that it would take generations to accumulate.

'After all, the police think Miss Aitchison's death was brought about by purely material means – a high heel, a long skirt, and a flight of stone steps that broke her neck. Nothing particularly mysterious about that – except for Beth Chase's testimony, and a girl of thirteen is not too reliable as a witness. I'm convinced that there is mischief afoot at Brereton – but I'm not yet convinced that it is disembodied mischief. And that reminds me – have you made your will?'

Faustina let her breath out in a long sigh of deflation. 'No.'

'Why not?'

She shrugged. 'You know I haven't any family. I can't think of anyone who would care to inherit my few belongings.'

'Then choose someone at random – a casual acquaintance, anybody. You can always change your will later, if you marry or form new friendships. But no one who appears to be threatened from an unknown source should risk dying intestate. That way, you have no idea who may profit by your death.'

Faustina smiled wanly. 'If I had property, that would be true. As it is, no one is going to profit much whether I die intestate or not.'

'Tomorrow I shall see your Mr Watkins and find out if he knows anything about your family connexions even though he keeps such outlandish office hours that I'll have to get up at five a.m. Then I'll call you here tomorrow evening and . . .'

'But I shall not be here tomorrow evening.'

'Why not?'

'I need rest and privacy. I must get away from these reporters and I had already planned to go down to my cottage at Brightsea tomorrow for the rest of the winter.'

'Don't.' Basil spoke sharply. 'Not yet. If you don't like this hotel, find another. But do stay in a hotel – a big, bright, noisy hotel like this, with plenty of doormen and elevator men. Use the main dining-room for meals. Don't go off by yourself. Stay in crowds. And please lock your door at night until you hear from me again.'

'Lock my door?' Faustina's laughter rang dry and cracked. 'Do you think a locked door would make any difference to . . . ?'

'To what?' He forced her to go on, believing it would be cathartic for her mind to drag its worst fears into words.

'Can't you guess what I'm afraid of?'

'Tell me.'

'I'm afraid of seeing the – thing myself. As Goethe did.'

'Then you've never seen it yourself?'

'Only once, and that was only a glimpse. Now I'm no longer sure what I saw. It was the night I left Brereton. I was standing at the head of the front stairs. Mrs Lightfoot was below me. I seemed to see a sort of movement among the shadows at the foot of the stairs – nothing more. But Mrs Lightfoot's behaviour made me suspect that she had seen more. Whatever it was, it – disturbed her.'

'And you?'

'I wasn't too frightened. If there were never anything more than that, I could bear it. Just a movement in the shadows beyond the light . . . I could even bear seeing the back of a figure that resembled mine at a distance, in a dim light, for a few moments, with other people around me. That could be anything or nothing – say, an optical delusion. I could even bear it if I saw the face of the figure, fleetingly, at a distance. That, too, could be some trick or illusion. But – suppose it doesn't stop there?'

'What else could happen?'

'Don't you really understand?'

Faustina's voice was low and throbbing. Her slim hands gripped the arms of her chair in sudden tension. 'Suppose, some day, or some night, when I'm quite alone in my own room, with all the lights turned on and the door locked, I should suddenly see a figure and a face close to mine and recognize it as my own face, feature for feature, in every detail and every flaw, even this pimple on my left cheek. That couldn't be fake or illusion. If that happened, I'd finally be sure that I, or some part of me, was travelling in undiscovered country.

' . . . I wouldn't know how I got there, or why I went there, or what I did there . . . I would only know that I was there . . . And I'd be afraid of the unknown within myself. Can you imagine the mortal shock? Then I'd know it was real and believe I should die . . .'

'Don't dwell on that idea.' Basil put all the firmness at his command into his voice. 'That cannot happen and you know it.'

But he was more honest with himself than most men of scientific education. As he stepped into the street a few moments later he looked up at the watchful stars – bright, silent, impersonal, and unimaginably far away if the astronomers' guesswork had any basis in reality. At his university he had been taught that the black distance was immeasurably cold the farther it was from the earth. Now, later researches had revealed alternate layers of cold and heat as far as thermometers could be sent. No one knew why it wasn't all cold, as it was supposed to be.

He shivered and turned up his coat collar. His heels rang sharply on the pavement through the cold, still night. As he walked to the corner he muttered half aloud: 'Who am I to say what cannot happen in this unknowable world?'

CHAPTER TEN

For in the time we know not of
Did Fate begin
Weaving the web of days that wove
Your doom, Faustine.

Juniper's reluctant tap on the door woke Basil from a few hours' fitful sleep. Anathematizing the eccentric office hours of Septimus Watkins, he dragged himself out of bed, still sleepy, and forced his shrinking flesh into a cold shower that roused him without refreshing him. A low, dark sky blotted out the dawn. A ground mist, rolling in from the East River, veiled the city in ragged streamers of white vapour as he walked two blocks to the Third Avenue garage where he kept his car.

He knew Watkins only by reputation. The man was one of those lawyers who never appear in court, yet for over fifty years he had served as counsellor and confidential agent to half the great fortunes of New York. He administered their trust funds, drew up their marriage and divorce settlements, executed their wills, and stood guard over their investment portfolios. He was so widely known and so rarely seen that he had become a tradition, almost a legend. Innumerable anecdotes illustrated the tough suppleness of his mind and the shrewdness of his worldly judgement. But, like most people, Basil had no idea what the man behind the myth was really like.

At ten minutes to six the lobby of the great office building at the corner of Broad and Wall was empty except for an elevator man and a scrubwoman who was wearily dragging a dirty mop across a mosaic floor inlaid with brass. When Basil reached the twenty-sixth floor there was no light behind the double doors of ground glass lettered *Watkins, Fisher, Underwood, Van Arsdale, and Travers.* He tried the handles. Both doors were locked. He found a small button in the jamb and pressed it. After his fourth ring, he began to wonder if Watkins misled people deliberately about his habits – an ingenious way of discouraging visitors. He was turning away when the glass glowed yellow and the door was thrown open by a slight, agile man. His hair was white, but thick and springy, the cheeks below it round and pink. He looked like a man in middle age whose hair had turned white prematurely. Septimus Watkins was over seventy.

'I understand Mr Watkins is here at this hour?' Basil was still not quite able to believe in such unconventional office hours. 'Will you please tell him that Dr Willing is here?'

'I'm Watkins. Come in, won't you?' He spoke without ceremony. 'You must be Basil Willing, the psychiatrist?' The blue eyes were sharp, but not unfriendly. 'My office is down the hall. This way.'

They passed through a reception room, large as the lobby of a small hotel. Watkins led the way down a long corridor with closed doors on either side, through three private offices, each large, dark, and empty. At last he threw open another door. They entered a corner office, larger than all the others, with windows on two sides giving a magnificent view of the harbour. The sickly November sun was just struggling above the white mist that still blurred the skyscrapers.

Basil paused before a fireplace of tawny marble where yellow tongues of flame licked lazily at a pile of birch logs, taking the edge off the morning chill. 'I haven't seen a wood fire in an office since I was in London. Do you serve tea here at five o'clock?'

Watkins's smile was cordial, frank, unhesitating – the smile of a man who had not been rebuffed or outwitted for many years. 'I believe in being comfortable, wherever I am. I don't care for tea, but there's a small bar behind that panel if you care to press the button.'

'No, thank you.' Basil's glance went back to the window-panorama of the world's greatest seaport. 'No wonder you come here so early. If I were you, I'd live here!'

'That's not why I am here so early.' The blue eyes twinkled. 'You must have wondered about that. I'll explain. Many years ago, when my practice was smaller, I discovered that a man with an office is constantly hampered by time-wasters. A tough receptionist can take care of obvious pests. Men selling insurance, women selling silk stockings, self-styled philanthropists soliciting for organized charity, and just plain bums asking for handouts. She can even stand off reporters and district leaders and crackpots and con men. But what are you going to do about your own clients and your own partners when they just want to sit and talk? You can't work while they're there, but you have no work if they're not there at all.

'At last I hit on this scheme. I decided to keep peculiar office hours. Every weekday I would be in my office but only from six to seven a.m. I would never refuse to see anyone who asked to see me personally, no matter who he was and what his business or lack of business. But – and this is a big "but" – in order to see me, he would have to be in my office by six in the morning, which generally meant he would have to get up at four-thirty or five. From what I had seen of human nature, I suspected that no one would get up that early in the morning just to see me unless he had something really important to say to me.'

'And you were right?'

'In the last twenty-three years, only twice have I had my time wasted by long-winded visitors with nothing to say. And I didn't really mind those two. I felt that if they wanted to waste their time so badly they were willing to get up at five a.m. to do so, they deserved a little of my time.

'Most people, when they hear they have to get here by six if they want to catch me, decide that they would rather see one of my partners at a more reasonable hour and let him relay the facts of the case to me. You'd really be surprised how few visitors I have, but I still make it a point of honour never to refuse anyone a personal interview providing he will take the trouble to come at this hour. And I really believe I get more work done here in one hour without interruptions than I could do in eight hours with a constant stream of visitors. Of course, the telephone is disconnected until I leave at seven and whatever work is unfinished I take home with me.'

Basil smiled ruefully. 'Well, Mr Watkins, I shall try not to be long-winded, but I'm afraid you are going to count me as the third visitor in twenty-three years who came at six with nothing important to say. That is, nothing of importance to you. Naturally it's important to me, or I wouldn't be here.'

Watkins laughed. 'That is the whole point. If it's important to you, I'm willing to listen. What I objected to were people who bothered me about things that weren't important even to them, just for the pleasure of hearing themselves talk. Please sit down and tell me what's on your mind.'

Basil sat with his back to the fire, facing a window. 'You – or at least your firm – are acting as trustee for Miss Faustina Crayle. I want to know who will inherit her property in the event of her death.'

The pleasant twinkle faded from Watkins's eyes. 'That is not the kind of information lawyers give to casual inquirers.'

'I'm not precisely a casual inquirer. I'm medical assistant to the district attorney and a friend of Miss Crayle's. Do you know anything about the circumstances of her leaving Brereton?'

'I know that she has left,' replied Watkins cautiously. 'She didn't tell me the reason. In any case, it shouldn't matter very much to her. She will inherit a tidy little nest-egg on her thirtieth birthday next fall. Her property is safeguarded in every way.'

'I am not thinking of her property,' answered Basil. 'I am thinking of her sanity, perhaps her life.'

'Did she consult you as a psychiatrist?'

'She is not a patient of mine. She consulted me as a friend. But, as a psychiatrist, I cannot help realizing how her situation may affect her mental health. Hasn't it occurred to you that there was something odd about the fact that she lost two teaching jobs two years in succession? Each a few weeks after school opened? Each involving the breaking of a contract?'

'As Miss Crayle's only guardian I should like to hear the details of her difficulties. Or would you be violating a confidence if you told me?'

'I think not. In any case, I should be willing to violate a confidence if that would save Miss Crayle.'

'Save Miss Crayle? From what?'

'Perhaps you can tell me.' Briefly Basil summarized Faustina's experiences at Maidstone and Brereton.

Watkins listened attentively, without comment. When Basil had finished, there was a suspended moment before Watkins roused himself to reply.

'An amazing story, Dr Willing. I am too old – I have seen too many strange things – to dismiss all this as schoolgirl hysteria. That doesn't mean that I accept an extra-human explanation. I don't know what to think.'

'Neither do I. But there is always the possibility that someone has a motive for driving Miss Crayle to suicide or insanity. That motive might be rooted in psychopathic malice or it might spring from the most material thing in the world – property.'

'Or both.'

'Do you know Miss Crayle's heir, or heirs?'

'I do. There's only one.'

'Who is it?'

'Myself.' Watkins smiled at Basil's astonishment. 'I'm not being entirely frank with you,' he went on. 'Legally, I am Miss Crayle's heir. According to her mother's will, if Miss Crayle dies before her thirtieth birthday, I inherit some jewels that would otherwise go to Miss Crayle. But her mother made an informal verbal agreement with me that I was to pass the jewels along to certain other people whom she did not wish to mention by name in her will.'

'Will you name them to me?'

'I'm sorry. I can't.'

'Would you name them to Miss Crayle herself?'

Watkins allowed his eyes to wander toward the nearest window.

The steeple of Old Trinity looked dark and dwarfish far below the grey stone battlements of high finance. 'I can't even do that. You see, Miss Crayle's circumstances are extraordinary. I'm going to tell you what I can because I believe that it is the quickest way to disabuse your mind of the preposterous notion that any threat to Miss Crayle can come from – from this direction. But I must withhold names. And I must ask you to keep all this confidential between us. I particularly do not want it repeated to Miss Crayle herself. I know you by reputation. I'm trusting you to be discreet in a delicate situation. And I'd rather tell you myself than have you probing into Miss Crayle's history.'

'So Miss Crayle has a history?'

Watkins's eyes narrowed and his lips puckered together in a centripetal grimace as if he were gathering together all his mental forces. 'That unfortunate girl, Faustina Crayle, is illegitimate. Her mother was – well, I believe it was Mr Kipling who first called it the "oldest profession in the world". Today we know more about prehistoric customs and we know that prostitution is one of the most modern professions. Where there is no property there is no marriage and where there is no marriage there is no vice.'

'Faustina's mother was a prostitute?' exclaimed Basil incredulously.

'More accurately a courtesan in the great tradition of Ninon de l'Enclos.' Watkins's smile was smaller and closer now, seeming to savour a scandal safely sterilized by time. 'Crayle was her real name. Professionally she was known as – by another name.'

'You won't tell me what it was?'

'I should prefer not to. She was born in Baltimore, the daughter of a man who wrote hymns. She had red hair. In the nineties she ran away from home – first to New York, then Paris. There she became a star of the *demi-monde* – one of those fabulous Parisian houris Balzac describes with such relish and detail. She was only a provincial American girl, yet from highly cultivated lovers she learned to speak and write perfect French, to understand music, art, and letters . . . Oh, it's impossible to make an American of your generation understand! Only Paris in the nineteenth century and Athens in the Periclean age have produced such women. The true *demi-mondaine* – who had everything the most distinguished *mondaine* could have except one thing – legal marriage and the status among other women that goes with it. She had a better life than any respectable woman living outside the world of fashion. She had wealth, a brilliant social life, the affection and even the respect of her lovers. In our time, my dear young man, even vice had a refinement that your generation will never see again. I tell you she was a courtesan and what does that convey to your twentieth-century mind? Bleached hair, blood-red nails, and a disgusting slang word – "floozy". This woman had a mind. And manners.'

'And the father?' put in Basil.

'The man was a New Yorker, with a fortune invested in shipping. In 1912 he wanted a divorce without accusing his wife publicly, so he went to Paris and let himself be seen once driving in the Bois with this woman. At that time she was so notorious on both sides of the ocean that a single drive in an open carriage with her was held by a shocked American court to be adequate proof of adultery. Witnesses were imported from France and the wife was able to secure the divorce her husband wanted.

'It was common gossip that he paid the co-respondent a thousand dollars for the privilege of that public drive and the use of her name in court. She stipulated that they should part at her door-step without his so much as kissing her fingertips, but . . .' Again came that small, salacious smile. 'Faustina Crayle is the daughter of these two.'

'Then they didn't part on her doorstep . . . ?'

'Oh, yes, they did – that time. But an extraordinary thing happened. Or perhaps it wasn't so extraordinary. Perhaps she knew her trade. Perhaps it was part of her technique to maintain such great reserve during that first drive. You see, he meant her to be a mere convenience, a pretext for divorce. She may have resented that and taken her revenge. In any case, this woman, who was to have been a convenience, altered the whole course of the man's life, for he fell in love with her. You find that hard to believe? I don't. Her years in Paris had given her a polished wit and she was a most beautiful woman then – hair like fire, skin like snow, and the body of Botticelli's Aphrodite . . .'

'You knew her in those days?' Basil spoke before he realized that the verb had several meanings in this context.

'I – I had that privilege.' Watkins responded almost primly, but there was an unmistakable spark in his old eyes. 'I was the man's lawyer, among other things.'

'And this is the origin of that shy, anaemic, day-dreaming girl!' Basil was rearranging every idea he had ever had about Faustina.

Watkins's shoulders sketched a shrug. 'We used to have a saying – the daughter of a flirt is always a prude.'

'Has she no suspicion of the truth?'

'I think not. As her guardian, I carried out the wishes of both parents and kept all knowledge of it from her. That is why I do not wish you to repeat this to Faustina. She is conventional and sensitive. It would break a spirit that has never been self-assertive.'

'Did her mother fall in love with – this man?'

The old eyes clouded, looking beyond the harbour view. 'What man could ever understand such a woman? You didn't want to understand her. You simply enjoyed her.' Again Basil noticed a choice of verb that left actual meaning ambiguous.

'He brought her back to America,' went on Watkins. 'He gave her a little house in Manhattan – people didn't have apartments then – and a summer cottage in New Jersey that had belonged to him for a number of years. He had his divorce, but – he didn't marry her. Not even when she became pregnant.'

'Why not?'

'My dear boy, this began in 1912. Men of that generation didn't marry that kind of woman. Today, I suppose he would have married her. Your generation has blurred all dividing lines. You don't even call them *demi-mondaines*. You call them hostesses or models or starlets and you marry them without thinking twice about it. Your one term of reproach, "floozy", is usually preceded by the adjective "cheap" and you apply it only to the bedraggled, unsuccessful whore. Your generation tolerates any moral lapse, but it cannot forgive economic failure.'

'Didn't your generation create wickedness artificially by drawing that sharp line between Eve and Lilith?' suggested Basil. 'Just so you could enjoy the thrill of feeling utterly depraved? We're more realistic and less unkind.'

'Possibly. I'm too submerged in old ideas to analyse them. Certainly our conventions have made poor Faustina suffer for something she never knew or understood. She was born in 1918.

Her mother was forty-three, the father already in his fifties. He knew he had not long to live. A heart condition which Faustina has inherited. He wanted to provide for the little girl and her ill-famed mother without any unpleasant publicity that might affect the child's future. He consulted me and I pointed out that he could not mention either the mother or the girl in his will without scandal, since there were other legitimate heirs by the divorced wife, who would contest any provision for the mistress. I suggested an outright gift to be made before his death – the kind of thing we do nowadays to evade inheritance taxes. Unfortunately just the day before he was to sign the deed he had a heart attack and died, leaving Faustina's mother with nothing but the two houses and some jewels.

'She came to me for advice. We kept the New Jersey cottage as a permanent home and sold the town house. Its sale brought in enough money to provide for Faustina's education and living expenses. I advised against selling the jewels at that time, for I was sure they would appreciate in value, as they have. Today they should bring in a neat sum for Faustina.'

'What do you call a neat sum.'

'A matter of some twenty or thirty thousand dollars. I cannot be more definite, because I haven't had the stones valued recently and the market is fluctuating. There is a pair of ruby earrings that should be worth a great deal more than they were forty years ago – just how much I don't know. Those jewels were the only capital Faustina's mother had to leave her daughter. The mother was afraid the girl might lose or waste her only resource through inexperience and therefore insisted that I draw up a will reserving the inheritance until Faustina's thirtieth birthday. That raised the question you have been asking me: Who was to get the jewels if both mother and daughter died before Faustina reached the age of thirty?

'When I put that question to the mother she was silent for a long time. Then she said: "I have trusted you for many years. Now I am going to give you a last trust. Something I planned long ago. There are some names I cannot put into a will. To do so would cause pain to everyone concerned when the will was probated. So in my legal, public will, I shall leave the jewels to you. But, privately, I am going to give you a list of names. Opposite each name will be the description of certain particular pieces of jewellery. If I and my daughter both die before she is old enough to inherit these things, I want you to promise me that you will give each piece to the man named beside it on this list or to his heirs. And that you will do so as discreetly as possible."

'It was most irregular, of course. But the whole situation was irregular. I saw at once what she was getting at – the list of names was a roster of her lovers, the men who had given her the jewels in the first place. Many of them were, doubtless, family jewels and her romantic conscience was bothering her in her old age. If Faustina couldn't have these things, her mother wanted them to go back to the wives and daughters and granddaughters who had a sentimental right to them.

'In order to protect my own reputation, I sent the mother to another lawyer and he drew up a will naming me as her heir if Faustina died before thirty. Today I still have that list in my safe. If I should inherit the jewels, I shall give them to the heirs of the men named and then burn the list.' He laughed. 'You see, I have more than one use for a wood fire in my office!'

'I'm sure you do.' Basil thought of all the scandalous secrets that must be stored under the thatch of thick white hair. 'How many people have seen this list?'

'No one except Faustina's mother and myself. It is in a manila envelope, sealed with an impression of her own thumb in red wax. As she has been dead many years that seal could not be duplicated easily.'

'How many people know about the list?'

'I have never mentioned it to anyone but you.'

'I have just one more question: What are the names on the list?'

Watkins's answer was quick and incisive. 'My dear Dr Willing, that I am not at liberty to tell you. I cannot betray the woman's trust in me and I cannot smirch the eminently respectable families involved in this old, forgotten scandal. But I give you my personal assurance that they are not the sort of people from whom Faustina Crayle need fear trickery or violence.'

'Can you say that any sort of people will not resort to trickery or violence under pressure?' retorted Basil. 'All this happened a long time ago. Family fortunes can alter surprisingly fast. Today some of these families may be in actual need of ready money – even a few thousand. And the jewels may be more valuable than you think.'

'I doubt if any single family on the list would receive more than five or ten thousand, at the most.'

'What if several men on the list have died without leaving heirs? If only one or two families remain, wouldn't they receive a considerable fortune in jewels? A sum big enough to give an unbalanced mind already predisposed toward violence that final extra push that sends a man or woman over the edge of the law?'

'The sum would be substantially increased if there were only one or two heirs – naturally,' admitted Watkins. 'But why do you postulate an unbalanced mind?'

'If anyone is playing some sort of trick on Miss Crayle, the mind that conceived it is unbalanced. Women like her mother provoke a sadistic rage in such minds – a rage that might even extend to the daughter.'

'You forget one thing,' returned Watkins. 'The seal on the envelope is intact, and I have never mentioned the list to anyone but you. Not even to Faustina herself. For if I had she would certainly have suspected the truth and probably have ferreted out the whole story of her origin. Therefore none of these families can possibly know their names occur on such a list.'

'Are you sure? The mother herself may have told one of the men named on the list all about it before her death. And he may have told others – especially his heirs.'

'I doubt if Faustina's mother would have been so foolish. I hope not.'

'So do I.'

'Dr Willing, you have not used the word "murder". But you have implied it. Let's speak more plainly. Murderers are practical. They don't call attention to their purposes by staging an elaborate hoax for over a year before the fact. Do they?'

'I don't know and – neither do you.' Basil's tone blunted the sharpness of his retort. 'What if I should make a police matter of this list?'

'I sincerely trust you will not do anything so absurd after you've had time to think it over. Nothing has happened to Faustina that suggests she is in any physical danger.'

Basil rose to take his leave, then paused. 'Mr Watkins, perhaps you'll give me a small hint. Do any of these names occur on that list: Lightfoot? Chase? Vining? Murphy? Maidstone? Aitchison?'

'No lawyer would answer such a question.'

But, as Basil left the room, Watkins was still frowning. Something had disturbed him.

CHAPTER ELEVEN

What ghosts unclean
Swarmed round the straitened, barren bed
That hid Faustine?

Twilight was melting into night when Basil came home that evening after a day at the psychiatric clinic. Before the war the narrow house on lower Park Avenue had seemed a poor substitute for his childhood home in Baltimore. Now, after years overseas, it was home and always would be. He had come to love the neighbourhood, especially at this hour – the river of cars flowing uptown with a steady whispering of tyres, the soft bloom of curtained lamplight in low, old-fashioned houses on either side of the wide, old-fashioned street, the glitter of the Grand Central building, a lighted transparency pasted against the rich blue of the night sky. After a day of work that demanded close, constant attention, it was luxury to relax in the comfortable knowledge that as soon as Juniper heard the latchkey in the lock he would start mixing the pre-dinner Martini.

Only tonight it didn't happen that way.

Basil was crossing the chessboard floor of black-and-white marble in the vestibule when the inner door opened cautiously. Juniper's wrinkled brown face appeared in the opening. 'Folks waitin' in the liberry, Dr Willing,' he whispered. 'Mr and Mrs

Chase and Mr Vining. Want to slip upstairs? I could say you phoned you weren't coming home.'

'No, thanks.' Basil forgot that he had felt tired a moment ago. This new development quickened his flagging energies.

He went up the flight of wide, shallow steps to the long white-panelled library that was also living-room and study. Juniper had drawn the cranberry-red curtains and lighted the white-shaded lamps. At the sound of Basil's footsteps, a young man turned swiftly toward the open archway. Lamplight flowed over his head, pointing up golden highlights in ash-blond hair that curled crisply close to his small head.

'Dr Willing? Please forgive this intrusion, but the matter is urgent. I am Raymond Vining, Margaret's brother. Mrs Lightfoot suggested that I should consult you. I took the liberty of bringing Mr and Mrs Chase with me. They are Elizabeth's parents.'

Elizabeth? Margaret? It took Basil an instant to recognize in these resounding names the two little girls, Beth and Meg, who had told him about their simultaneous vision of Faustina and her double at Brereton.

The other man and the woman were in shadow beyond the lamplight. She sat in an armchair near the empty hearth, her face masked by the eccentric shadow of a modern hat. Her dark clothes blended with the dim background; the light caught only the glossy fur about her shoulders, and the green fire of emeralds on her small gnarled hands. The man stood with his back to the fireplace, his legs spread wide apart, a short burly figure with something truculent in its stance, and a bald head that shone greasily as if it had been rubbed with wax.

As Basil stood in the archway he caught the ghost of a familiar fragrance – lemon verbena. It was gone before he reached the centre of the room. He could not tell which of the three had brought it here.

Dorothea Chase was speaking querulously. 'Mrs Lightfoot told us that you knew more about this extraordinary business at Brereton than anyone else. I wish to know if you think I should withdraw Elizabeth from the school?'

'I think Beth should leave that place at once,' put in Chase. 'I hope you agree with me, Dr Willing. I can't do much about it myself. We're divorced and Dorothea has custody.'

'I've about decided to take Meg away from that school,' added Vining. 'But I want a clearer idea of what's been happening to her there. I'm worried.'

He didn't look worried. He was standing negligently with one arm resting on a bookcase. He had the narrow face and long-legged, hipless figure that Victorian novelists called 'aristocratic'. Basil had seen the same leanness too often in the families of farmers and factory workers to believe that the human bone structure can be altered in a few generations by property and leisure.

'But it's such a delightful school!' Dorothea spoke petulantly. 'Floyd – my husband – doesn't understand what a tremendous advantage it is for Elizabeth to be thrown with the sort of girl she meets there. If I take her away now it may alter the whole course of her life.'

'There are other schools, aren't there?' snapped Chase.

'There's only one Brereton and you know it. It is to America what Roedean is to England.'

'Well, it won't be much longer. Not after this!'

'Mrs Lightfoot told us that dreadful Miss Crayle was gone for good.'

Vining intervened. 'Was she so dreadful, this Miss Crayle? I don't yet understand the part she played in the peculiar stories Meg relayed to me. Tell us, Dr Willing, was Miss Crayle the agent or the victim?'

Basil answered gravely: 'The victim seems to have been Alice Aitchison.'

There was a moment of silence, loaded, heavy, and tight. Dorothea was the first to rally. 'What on earth do you mean? Surely that was an accident?'

'An accident that occurred when Miss Aitchison saw Miss Crayle at a time and place where it was impossible for her to be,' went on Basil. 'At least, that is your daughter's story. It may be accident that a fall killed Miss Aitchison, but what made her fall? The fact that she saw Miss Crayle under circumstances which made that sight a great shock to her?'

'Do you mean that Miss Crayle was deliberately trying to frighten Miss Aitchison?' asked Vining.

'Apparently it wasn't Miss Crayle at all,' answered Basil. 'She is able to prove that she was in New York at the time.'

'Then who was it?' cried Chase. 'What in hell happened anyway?'

For answer, Basil crossed the room to the shelf where he kept books venturing into the farthest frontiers of abnormal psychology, and even beyond them. He took down a book bound in dingy brown cloth, published almost exactly a hundred years ago, in 1847. He came back to the reading lamp beside the fireplace and opened the book.

'Here is something that is supposed to have happened in Livonia in 1845, to a girl named Emilie Sagée. It has been published many times since, in various versions, by Guldenstubbe, by Owen, by Aksakoff, by Flammarion.'

He began to read aloud from yellow pages with crumbling brown edges. As he read, stillness grew around him. He had a feeling that the nerves of his auditors were strung to a humming tautness, almost at breaking-point.

The story he read was curiously parallel to the story of Faustina Crayle, only the girls' school was at Volmar, fifty-eight miles from Riga, and the teacher was a French girl from Dijon – frail and gentle, thirty-two years old. At first there were simply stories that Mademoiselle Sagée had been seen in two different places by different people when there hadn't been time for her to get from one place to the other. Stories that led to arguments among the witnesses, the mutual charges of malobservation. But at last something happened that couldn't be explained so easily. Two identical figures of her were seen simultaneously by an embroidery class of forty-two girls – one figure appearing for several minutes in a chair in the classroom while the other figure could be seen just outside the window gathering flowers in the garden. As long as the appearance remained in the chair, the girl outside the window moved 'slowly and heavily, like a person overcome with sleep or fatigue'.

'Why, that's just what Beth said about the Crayle woman,' muttered Chase.

Basil closed the book and looked at his audience. Dorothea Chase sat far back in the shadows of her chair, her jewelled hands resting still in her lap. Only her mouth was visible – a pout painted scarlet. Chase's forefinger fumbled at a thin line of moustache on his full upper lip. His eyes were serious and puzzled. Vining still leaned gracefully against the bookcase. But though his posture was the same, his attitude had undergone a subtle change. He was listening intently, as if he must not miss a word of this. His eyes were like his little sister's – a bright blue that seemed oddly misted, like a star sapphire.

'There were other appearances, even more curious,' continued Basil. 'Finally all but twelve of the forty-two girls at the school were removed by their parents and Mademoiselle Sagée was dismissed. On that occasion she is said to have wept and cried out: "This is the nineteenth time since my sixteenth year that I have lost a position because of this!" From that moment when she walked out of the Neuwelcke School, she vanished from history. What became of her, no one knows. But one of the pupils, thirteen-year-old Baroness Julie von Guldenstubbe, told the tale to a brother who had dabbled in psychic research. Through him, it entered the literature on the subject and became for a few students the classic case of the double or *doppelgänger*, though it has remained unknown to the general public to this day.

'In 1895, Flammarion, finding himself in Dijon, was curious enough to look at the birth records for 1813 which must have been the year of Mademoiselle Sagée's birth if she was really thirty-two in 1845. There was no Sagée family mentioned in the records for that year. But on 13 January 1813 an infant girl was born in Dijon named Octavie Saget. In French, of course, Sagée and Saget are pronounced the same way. Anyone who heard the name without reading it would not know which way it was spelled, especially a girl of thirteen who was not French herself, like Julie von Guldenstubbe. It seems less likely that she could have mistaken "Octavie" for "Emilie". But in the birth record after the name "Octavie Saget" there appeared a single word which may have some significance, the word: *illegitimate.*

'Irregular birth might account for the wandering life of exile which Emilie Sagée, or Octavie Saget, seems to have led as a French teacher in Germany and Russia. Dijon is a small provincial town. No people are more prudish and conventional than provincial French, and they were especially so in the nineteenth century. Conceivably Emilie Sagée may have connived at the varied spelling of her last name and the alteration of her first name in an effort to conceal her origin. And if there was any psychopathic basis for the apparently inexplicable happenings at Neuwelcke, it may have been rooted in the mental disintegration of a sensitive girl under the emotional burden of illegitimacy. That, of course, is pure speculation . . .'

Dorothea stirred and turned her head. Now the lamplight fell across her face. Under the cosmetic mask Basil saw the special uneasiness of the frivolous woman forced into seriousness against her will.

'Really, Dr Willing!' Her incredulity was reinforced by a keen sense of what is and is not done. 'Are you asking us to believe that Miss Crayle and this French girl really did produce a sort of phantom? It's preposterous and' – she sought for a word and came up triumphantly with – 'impractical!'

'There is one extremely practical point about all this,' answered Basil.

'Really?' Vining was gently ironic. 'What is it?'

'The exact parallel between the two cases. The Crayle case is actually a plagiarism of the Sagée case in every detail.'

'Except for the illegitimacy,' murmured Vining.

Dorothea was watching Basil's face. 'I don't suppose Miss Crayle is illegitimate, is she?'

Basil ignored the question. 'Suppose someone who wished to injure Miss Crayle happened to read or hear the story of Mademoiselle Sagée and decided to re-enact it for that purpose. That would explain the close parallel between the two.'

'But how could it injure Miss Crayle?' demanded Vining.

'It has already cost her two jobs.'

'Two?' Dorothea was surprised.

'Yes. What is worse, I believe it is shattering her mental health. It might drive her to – almost anything. There is only one incident that doesn't fit the Sagée pattern – the death of Miss Aitchison. Unless Miss Aitchison somehow got in the way of some effect that was aimed at Miss Crayle.'

'I suppose you mean that the appearance of the double at Brereton after Miss Crayle had left was designed to frighten Miss Crayle, who was sure to hear about it,' said Vining. 'It was planned to startle whoever happened to see it. But it wasn't planned that anyone should be startled enough to fall down a flight of stone steps and break her neck. That really was an accident.'

Chase's mind moved more slowly than Vining's. 'Let me get this straight, Ray. You mean this double thing is just a fake of some sort?'

'Naturally.' Vining was impatient.

'But then . . .' Chase looked from Vining to Basil and back to Vining again. 'How was it done? How could anyone fake an appearance of Miss Crayle that looked real enough to frighten Alice when she saw it face to face in broad daylight.'

Vining passed the question on to Basil. 'Well?'

Basil sighed. 'I wish I knew.'

'If this figure was exactly like Miss Crayle, I suppose it was done with some sort of reflector,' suggested Dorothea.

'When Miss Crayle was sketching on the lawn outside the house and the double was sitting in an armchair inside the house?' Basil shook his head. 'According to your own daughter, Miss Crayle and the image looked exactly alike, but they were not doing the same thing at the same time. No reflector could create that illusion.'

'That is damned queer,' admitted Chase, reluctantly. 'All along I've been thinking of mirrors. Is there any way to project a moving picture without a screen?'

'And in bright sunshine?' Vining laughed. 'I'm afraid not, Floyd. Besides, I can't visualize anyone carrying around a lot of machinery at Brereton and getting away with it. There's no privacy in a boarding school.'

'Well, then, what was it?' demanded Chase. 'There must have been something.'

'I cannot even suggest an explanation,' said Basil. 'Just as I think I've got one, I come across some detail that doesn't fit. On one occasion the so-called double seemed to carry out an impulse to pass Mrs Lightfoot on the stair that Miss Crayle herself had suppressed, as if the double were a visible projection of Miss Crayle's subconscious thought. I don't know how to account for that . . . Or for the slowness of Miss Crayle's voice when she was talking on the telephone at the very moment Miss Aitchison was dying . . .'

'Could she have been drugged then?' asked Chase.

'If she was, it must have been timed with remarkable accuracy,' answered Basil. 'If I were Mrs Lightfoot, I should be glad to see Elizabeth and Margaret leave the school, as well as Miss Crayle. And I should dismiss the maid, Arlene Murphy.'

Vining was annoyed. 'Are you suggesting that Meg . . . ?'

'Whatever the explanation, there must be a human factor at the bottom of it. If all those who were mixed up in it are separated, the thing may stop.'

'And it may not.' Vining spoke curtly. 'You've decided me, Dr Willing. My sister shall leave Brereton at once.'

'I don't know anything about abnormal psychology,' growled Chase. 'What's more, I don't want to know anything about it. But I do want Beth taken out of that school. You hear that, Dorothea? I'll go to court, if I have to!'

'Well . . .' Dorothea fingered her emeralds. 'Perhaps Partington would do next year. And I can get her a tutor for the rest of the winter. But it all seems so – so unpractical. What have you and I and Elizabeth got to do with something that happened in Livonia a hundred years ago?'

She rose, drawing on her gloves. The men followed her into the hall. There the glare from the chandelier overhead revealed her more clearly to Basil as the beauty-parlour product she was – henna-brown hair, brick-pink cheeks, scarlet lips and nails, black-encrusted lashes, and, underneath it all, the old, dry flesh kneaded and creamed and powdered. It was all so blatantly artificial that it reminded Basil of a quaint French farce he had seen long ago. A bride retired behind a screen to undress on her wedding night. First her clothes were tossed over the screen. Then a wig, false teeth and false eyelashes, glass eyes, artificial nails, a wooden arm, a wooden leg. At last the bridegroom tired of waiting, looked behind the screen and – there was nothing there. Just empty air and a heap of clothing on a bare floor. Was that piece of Gallic absurdity a symbol of what Floyd Chase's wedding night must have been?

Basil looked into Dorothea's eyes – the only thing on the whole visible surface of her body that was not doctored in some way. The iris was a light brown, curiously shallow and blank. It was like looking through a few inches of water to a dull, muddy river-bed. It told him nothing.

They were almost at the vestibule when Dorothea spoke to Vining, pointedly ignoring her former husband. 'My car is waiting. Will you drive uptown with me, Ray?'

'Love to.'

He followed her across the pavement to a dark limousine. A chauffeur opened the door.

Chase lingered beside Basil, hat in hand. 'I'd like a word with you alone.'

Basil looked at his watch. 'I'm meeting a friend at a restaurant.'

'Let me drive you there. We can talk on the way.'

Basil was about to refuse, but something baffled and pleading in Chase's expression changed the decision.

'All right. If you'll wait a moment while I leave the restaurant telephone number with Juniper. I may get a call from the hospital tonight.'

When Basil came back, Chase was standing at the kerb beside a rakish convertible, grey upholstered in bronze leather – just the sort of car he would have.

'What's troubling you?' asked Basil, as the car slid into traffic.

'Alice.' Chase kept his eyes on the glittering lights ahead of them.

'You mean Alice Aitchison? The young teacher who died at Brereton?'

'Yes. You see – I loved her.'

CHAPTER TWELVE

You'd give . . . poison, shall we say,
Or what, Faustine?

The restaurant was on Madison Avenue. Small, quiet, newly decorated, it served dishes that had a South American tang without the grease. But no celebrity had discovered it, so there were hardly any other diners. Some day Basil knew he would come here expecting dinner and find the floor space standing vacant, for rent again. Good food and pleasant surroundings were not enough. You needed ballyhoo, angles, front, and all the rest of it.

Gisela was sitting at a table in one of the booths. She had taken off her hat. The first thing Basil saw was the sweep of silky black hair above the pale delicate face. She had thrown back her beaver coat. Shoulders and waist were trim in grey, fastened to the throat with silver buttons. Pussywillow colours, he thought – dove-grey and warm brown with silvery highlights.

She looked up at him, smiling, and the hair fell away from her ears, revealing the long clean line of neck and chin. Then her glance went beyond him to the other man with a trace of surprise.

'Mr Chase is having a cocktail with us,' explained Basil. 'He needs one.'

'It's good of you to let me tag along.' Chase looked from one to the other with something like envy. 'I'll just have one drink and then I'll be off. The truth is, Miss von Hohenems, that I'm glad of a chance to talk to you as well as Dr Willing. It's about Alice. Did she tell you? About us?'

'Not in so many words,' responded Gisela. 'Though she did speak of leaving Brereton for good.'

The waiter took Basil's order. Chase waited until they were alone once more.

'That's what she meant,' he went on. 'I had asked her to marry me.'

'I suppose that's why she wore the orange housecoat,' suggested Gisela. 'She wanted to look her best for you and she didn't care what anyone else thought.'

'Possibly. Though, of course, I didn't care what she wore. I would have loved her in sackcloth . . . When I left Dorothea I swore I would never marry again. But Alice was everything Dorothea was not – gay, warm, vital, human . . .'

The waiter set three glasses before them. Chase took a sip indifferently, as if taste and every other sense were numb. 'That's why I was so sure from the first that it wasn't suicide. She was happy. I know she was. She wanted to live. And I have plenty of money – even with Dorothea taking all she can get and a little more. I could have given Alice everything she ever wanted. Now I can't get over the irony of the whole thing. That she should die in such a useless, stupid way on the very threshold of fulfilment.'

'Accidents . . .' began Gisela.

His glance stopped her. 'You know, it's quite a simple trick to break a human neck. They taught us how to do it in the Army. You put your hands in a certain position on either side of the head, you make a quick jerk sidewise and – the vertebra snaps.'

He was illustrating with both hands, fingers extended, palm facing palm, and a space for the imaginary head between them. The jerk had a grisly neatness and snap. He might have been demonstrating a salute or any other drill, 'to be executed in a smart, military manner . . .'

'Afterward, you could let the body fall down the steps. You could rip a hem and snatch off a shoe in a few seconds. And then who could say it wasn't an accident?'

Gisela gasped. 'But . . .'

Chase went on in a cheerless monotone. 'Three people hated her: Dorothea, my former wife, Raymond Vining, and Faustina Crayle. Dorothea was jealous and angry at the thought of my marrying again. Especially a young woman, like Alice, who might have children to inherit some of the money that would go to Beth otherwise. Ray Vining was engaged to Alice a year ago. A silly boy-and-girl affair, but I believe she jilted him. I know there was a quarrel of some sort. Alice had a rough side to her tongue. And I've been told she enjoyed baiting the Crayle girl.'

'Somehow I cannot visualize a woman breaking another woman's neck,' said Gisela. 'Women are more apt to use a gun or poison.'

'A jealous woman, in anger, will do anything,' retorted Chase. 'Even push another woman down a flight of stone steps. That's what Beth says Miss Crayle did to Alice . . . Did you notice anything, Miss von Hohenems? Anything you didn't tell the police?'

'No. I'm sorry, but there was nothing. Just Alice and the torn hem and the cast shoe.'

'Footprints?'

'I didn't see any. I suppose I wasn't looking for them then.'

He let out his breath as if he had been holding it for several seconds. 'All right, I suppose it was a forlorn hope – that we could ever find out how Alice really died.'

'You know Faustina was in New York at the time,' continued Gisela. 'I was talking to her on the telephone just before I found Alice.'

Chase set down his empty glass. 'The way I heard it, Miss Faustina Crayle is the one person in the world who can never have an alibi . . . God, I don't know what to believe! Thanks for the drink. I must be on my way. Good night.'

He stumbled to his feet, unsmiling, unseeing. He made a curt gesture of farewell and walked unsteadily down the aisle between the tables to the hat-check booth. He went blindly past the bowing headwaiter, through the doorway into the darkness.

Gisela looked at Basil. 'What do you think really happened to Alice?'

'I don't know.' Basil returned her gaze soberly. 'It's even possible that Chase himself killed her. He certainly demonstrated the method effectively just now. He may have been trying to find out from you if he had left any footprints or other telltale marks.'

'A lovers' quarrel?'

'Something of the sort. Have you any idea whether she really loved Chase or not?'

Gisela made a small grimace. 'You've seen him and you've seen Vining.'

'Vining would be more attractive to a woman?'

'I think so. Of course you cannot always be sure about these things. Some quite ugly men attract a certain type of woman. Male counterparts of the *belle laide* . . . But I can't help remembering that Chase is a wealthy man and that Alice was extremely tired of her life as a schoolteacher . . . How horrible if Beth Chase really saw something like that! Would a child that age be quick-witted enough to make use of the stories about Faustina to divert suspicion from her father? And were those stories about Faustina just illusion after all?'

Basil shook his head. 'It's not that simple, my dear. Mrs Lightfoot told me that Faustina was asked to leave the Maidstone school last year for the same reason.'

'Good Heavens, that was Alice's school!'

'Yes. And Alice enjoyed baiting Faustina.'

Gisela's eyes widened. 'You mean – Alice may have played some sort of malicious trick on Faustina, at both schools? A trick that cost Faustina two jobs. Then somehow Faustina found out and – came back to Brereton to punish Alice?'

'Then who talked to you on the long-distance telephone?'

'I know it was Faustina's voice.' Gisela frowned. 'I couldn't mistake that little, languid, faraway voice. And I know the call came from New York. The Connecticut police checked that with the telephone company.'

'Some people can mimic another person's voice with uncanny accuracy,' suggested Basil.

'I don't see Faustina taking another person into her confidence, do you?'

'Suppose she pretended it was all a hoax?'

'Then the other person would go straight to the police when the newspapers published the story of Alice's death. It must have been something else. Could a trick, played on Faustina by Alice, backfire in some way that would startle or shock Alice herself?'

'What trick? What could Alice actually do to produce Faustina's double? And how could that backfire?'

This time it was Gisela who shook her head.

'I've asked myself that question a dozen times,' went on Basil. 'Still, I'm unable to answer it. At Brereton the double was seen by four people: a rather stupid housemaid, two little girls of thirteen, and Mrs Lightfoot herself. The adult witnesses, the maid and Mrs Lightfoot, saw the double only when the light was dim. Neither one had a really good view of the face. Neither one saw the two figures simultaneously – Faustina herself and her fetch.'

'Fetch?'

'The old English word. Origin unknown. Perhaps the phantom double of a living person is called a "fetch" because its appearance is usually a warning of that person's death. It has come to fetch him. We still speak of a "fetching likeness". And you'll find the word in Dickens – the "very fetch and image of Mrs Gamp". Traditionally such an image appears in a dim light – at dusk, at dawn, by moonlight.'

'But this fetch or double was seen in broad daylight,' protested Gisela.

'Only twice – the first time by two little girls, the second time by one little girl. Whether Miss Aitchison saw anything or not, we shall never know. And on only one occasion was the double seen while Faustina herself was also in view. That incident, the strangest of all, also rests on the testimony of two little girls.'

'Why should they lie?' asked Gisela. 'They were really frightened. Beth did faint; Meg was white to the lips and shaking. And I, myself, saw how slowly Faustina moved at the time.'

'I don't believe they lied consciously,' answered Basil. 'But even adults see what they expect to see. Both girls had heard the stories about Faustina before they saw – whatever it was. Those stories may have prepared their minds so that they exaggerated the resemblance of the figure in the chair to the real Faustina.'

'And who – or what – was the figure in the chair? And why was it there? Was it the same figure seen at Maidstone a year ago?'

Basil sighed. 'I was tempted to go down to Virginia. But the incidents there occurred over a year ago. No one could be expected to recall details with any accuracy now and details are what we need – practical details about light, distance, clothing, and so forth. According to Faustina's own account, the double was seen at Maidstone in every kind of light – morning, afternoon, and evening – but always at a considerable distance.'

'Would anyone in the world carry on such a trick for over a year just to torment poor Faustina?'

'No normal person would do such a thing.'

'Would even an abnormal person have such a sad, industrious sense of humour?'

Basil smiled. 'The abnormal is in essence the unpredictable. Besides – what else could it be?'

There was a touch of whimsicality in Gisela's answering smile. 'In everything you say, you are assuming that this thing must be a trick. Will you – just for a moment – consider the possibility that there might be such a thing as an immaterial image of a living person, temporarily visible to other people? And that Faustina is one of the rare few who project such a human mirage unconsciously?'

'You've been talking to Mrs Lightfoot!'

'Yes, I have. And why not? She is a remarkably intelligent woman. Forget science and ask yourself if her hypothesis is not the only one that covers every point in Faustina's story without stretching or contriving?'

'Does it?' His smile was still sceptical.

But Gisela was in earnest now. 'It explains all the stories about Faustina at Maidstone and Brereton. And it explains Alice Aitchison's death. At Maidstone, she may have believed that the thing was a trick contrived by Faustina or someone else. When she found Faustina at Brereton, she wasn't tattletale enough to run to Mrs Lightfoot with the Maidstone story, but she treated Faustina with the mocking contempt a girl like Alice would feel for an hysteric or a trickster. Then Alice came face to face with an image of Faustina in broad daylight when Alice knew I was talking to the real Faustina on the telephone and the shock made her trip and fall. In that case, you see, little Beth Chase would be telling the truth. She saw exactly what happened.'

'Beth said that Faustina put out her hand toward Alice and pushed her.'

'That would make the shock to Alice all the greater if the image wasn't real.'

'Or if Alice thought it wasn't real,' amended Basil.

'You see?' Gisela laughed. 'You cannot surrender your mind to the idea that there might be such a thing! It's easier for me because I was brought up in Europe. An old civilization like ours is sceptical of all beliefs – even those modern, scientific beliefs for which you Americans have an almost religious reverence. We don't because our civilization has lived through so many intellectual revolutions. Again and again we have seen the science of one generation become the mythology of the next. We remember that the whole science of electricity is only about two hundred years old. And that, only ten years ago, reputable physicists were saying it would be impossible to split the atom. We know so well that saddest of old sayings: *This, too, will pass* . . .

'And the past is always with us, over there. In our customs and our homes, as well as our books. An ancient castle or fortress isn't just a place we've read about – often it's a place where people we know are still living. Strange things do happen in very old dwelling-places, like Wasserleonburg and Glamis. People who live in such places become so used to the unexplained that they lose all fear and even interest. You would be compelled to deny or investigate. We simply smile and shrug and say: *This, too, will pass* . . .'

'Are you asking me to believe that you would not be frightened if you came face to face with whatever Alice Aitchison saw? When you wrote me that first letter about Faustina you were not so bold!'

'That was before I knew what it was all about. The unknown is always terrifying. But now I do know – why should I fear any manifestation of a shy, harmless personality like Faustina Crayle's? If such things do exist, they are all part of nature for, of course, there is no such thing as the "super-natural". Whatever happens is natural, whether it's acceptable to science or not. Only dogmatic sceptics like Alice feel shock in such circumstances – the awful shock of a sudden cleavage between what you believe and what you see. I would not feel that shock because I have known other cases very like this one.'

'Have you ever had personal experience of such a thing?'

'Not I. But a great-aunt of mine – a Frenchwoman, Amalie de Boissy – had personal knowledge of something very like this. When her father was with the French Embassy in Russia, she was sent to school at a place called Volmar in Livonia.'

Basil looked up sharply. 'The Neuwelcke School?'

'You've heard of it?'

'I've heard of Emilie Sagée and the things that happened there. After all, psychiatry is my profession and every phase of abnormal psychology has a particular interest for me. Why haven't you mentioned Emilie Sagée before?'

'Do you recall the first time we talked about Faustina? That evening at the Crane Club? And how I told you I had an elusive memory of something similar? That was the Sagée story. I heard it long ago, when I was a very small girl. I suppose that's why it took me so long to remember it, though the Goethe incident should have reminded me. When Aunt Amalie first told me about Emilie Sagée she said something similar had happened once to the poet Goethe and she gave me her French edition of his *Memoirs* where he recounts the experience himself. As I recall the Sagée story, it was very like Faustina's except for one detail – Mademoiselle Sagée was illegitimate.'

Basil hesitated. Then, because he trusted Gisela as he trusted no one else, he went on: 'So was Faustina. But please don't mention that to anyone, ever. She is not supposed to know.'

'Oh – poor Faustina . . .' Gisela was moved. 'That explains why she always seemed so rootless and alone!'

'Her mother was notorious in Paris at the turn of the century. Under another name, not Crayle, her real name, which she gave to Faustina.'

'I have heard the professional name of such a woman recently. Just a few days ago . . . Why . . .' As recollection grew, Gisela became tense. 'It was Alice Aitchison who mentioned it to Faustina in my presence.'

'And the name?'

'Rosa Diamond. I've heard of her all my life as the queen of polite vice in Paris in 1900.'

Basil nodded. Rosa Diamond . . . The odd name seemed to reverberate through corridors of memory, waking long-dead echoes. 'Was she co-respondent in a celebrated divorce case in 1912?'

'I don't know.'

'Then that's something I must find out tomorrow. That and the name of the man in the case – if Rosa Diamond really was Faustina's mother.'

'If? She must have been. For only that would explain what Alice said. How cruel!'

'What did Alice say?'

'It was the day Faustina left Brereton for good. We were discussing a design Faustina had made for Medea's dress in the Greek play. Alice said Faustina had chosen a colour the Athenians reserved for prostitutes. Faustina protested that she hadn't known that. Alice laughed and said Faustina must know quite a lot about the traditions of prostitutes. And then Alice asked Faustina if she had ever heard of Rosa Diamond.'

'Think back before you answer this,' said Basil. 'And think carefully: did Faustina look as if she recognized the name Rosa Diamond?'

Gisela bent her head, pressing fingertips to either temple. At last she dropped her hands and looked up once more with baffled eyes. 'I honestly can't say. Everything Alice said that afternoon seemed to hurt Faustina. Does she know her mother's history?'

'Her lawyer says she knows nothing, but he may be mistaken. I'm afraid I shall have to ask Faustina herself about it.'

'How could Alice know about Faustina's mother?'

'That's something else I'll have to find out. How did your aunt know that Mademoiselle Sagée was illegitimate?'

'She didn't know; that side of the story was published long afterward by Flammarion and I read it there.'

'Did your aunt know Julie von Guldenstubbe?'

'No. You see my aunt went there thirteen years later – in 1858. None of the pupils who had been there with Mademoiselle Sagée were left. A few of the older servants who had known her remained. And the story was well known among the peasants of the neighbourhood at that time. It had become a tradition of the school. The sort of thing that girls whisper in dormitories, late at night, over a cup of chocolate brewed secretly when they're supposed to be in bed and asleep.'

Basil couldn't restrain a smile. 'Hardly the best method of arriving at the facts with absolute scientific accuracy!'

'I suppose not.' She answered his smile ruefully. 'But there's one detail that impressed me vividly when my aunt repeated the story to me, years later. The Sagée double appeared so often at Neuwelcke that, toward the end, the younger girls lost all fear of it.'

'You expect me to believe that?'

'It's not uncommon. That's what I've been trying to tell you. And it's especially apt to happen with children. They don't believe they're seeing the impossible because they have so little knowledge of what is considered possible. According to tradition, one little girl became bold enough to touch the double of Emilie Sagée.'

'And she felt . . . ?'

'Some say something filmy like chiffon. Some say nothing. You can't touch a mirage or a reflection, however plainly you may see it.'

'I should like to have known that little girl,' remarked Basil. 'She had the scientific spirit, and true courage.'

'Why should she fear something that always appeared silently and briefly, that never hurt anyone in any way? These shadowy things don't ever harm people. It's the people who harm themselves by their own superstitious fears!'

'How can you be sure?' retorted Basil. 'If such things could exist, it would all be undiscovered country. Anything could happen there. Remember, according to Beth Chase, it was when the double put out its hand that Alice Aitchison fell – to her death.'

Gisela lost a little of her assurance. Her dark eyes grew wide and troubled.

But Basil went on inexorably: 'You've just told me that Alice taunted Faustina with her mother's name. If Faustina understood that allusion, she must have had a hatred for Alice that was almost murderous . . .'

'Oh, no!'

'You know the chief accusation brought against witches in the Middle Ages?'

Gisela nodded miserably. 'The power to kill at a distance, invisibly? But I don't believe that!'

'Why not? You seem ready to believe things equally strange! Is only the pleasant aspect of such a thing believable? You've been speaking of the old world and its traditions. One you forget: *thou shalt not suffer a witch to live* . . . Myth and mystery always seem to end in cruelty and violence, Gilles de Rais and Torquemada. That may be one reason we of the new world offer such vehement resistance to any revival of these pre-scientific beliefs. We have racial memories of the torture chamber and the stake – the act of faith, the dark, still night desecrated by flames and the screams of the burning while the glassy eyes of believers reflect the red light of the fire . . .'

'You make it sound horrible.'

'It was horrible.'

'Your modern science burned thousands at Rotterdam and Coventry and Hiroshima while the Middle Ages only burned a few hundreds.'

'Does one crime excuse another?'

'Would you deny a thing you believed true because once, in the past, it had led to violence?'

'No more than I would deny science because men who were not scientists have misused it.'

The headwaiter was coming toward their table. He stopped with a smile. 'Dr Willing? A telephone call . . .'

Basil came back from the booth frowning. 'This is the very devil. Emergency meeting of the board at the hospital. The emergency is financial, so I'll have to go. They want figures that only I can supply. Estimated costs of new equipment for the psychiatric clinic. It would have to be this evening. There's always something . . .'

'Don't look so wretched! You're not going off to Japan this time.'

'I might as well be, for all the chance I have to see you now I'm back. At least, let me put you on the train to Brereton.'

'But I'm not going by train. For once, I have a car. Borrowed from another teacher. And I have a much better idea. Let me drive you to the hospital.'

It was only ten blocks. They both wished it had been farther. As he left the car, he bent his head to kiss the ungloved hand on the steering wheel – a tantalization. On the pavement, he turned to wave to her before he ran up the steps and through the double doors.

She sat still, the long evening stretching before her, empty as a desert. That emotional vacuum must be filled somehow . . . *Don't bother to call me . . . Just come any time you can . . . Friday or Saturday* . . . Abruptly, she spun the wheel and turned into a cross street, driving toward Fifth Avenue, where she recalled seeing a filling station.

A spatter of raindrops beaded the windshield. Even then she did not hesitate. Action was restoring her equilibrium. This was adventure. She would surprise Basil Willing. She might even force a breach in his indurated scepticism. And there was nothing to fear . . . Everything that happened was natural. It had to be or it couldn't happen.

A sleepy man in oil-stained overalls came through the garish light to the petrol pumps.

'Oil, too, please,' said Gisela. 'Have you a road map of New Jersey?'

'Sure. Any particular place?'

'I'm going to a little village by the ocean. It's called Brightsea.'

CHAPTER THIRTEEN

As if your fed sarcophagus
Spared flesh and skin,
You came back face to face with us,
The same Faustine.

The windshield wipers began their staccato ballet – one-two-three-kick – a pair of dancers, one-legged, abstract, moving in perfect unison. Through half-moons of clear glass, polished by their dancing, Gisela saw a blurred reflection of street lamps in the shimmering film of water that washed the black roadway. Inside the car she was in a small dry world of her own. The monotonous rhythm of the windshield wipers and the steady hum of the engine were having an almost hypnotic effect on eye and ear, lulling her to drowsiness . . .

Out of the blackness flashed a lighted signboard: YOU ARE NOW ENTERING THE VILLAGE OF BRIGHTSEA. The main highway was becoming the principal street of the village. The only lights came from a drugstore and a filling station. Gisela pulled into the filling station and stopped.

'Miss Crayle's cottage?' He was a lank countryman in jeans and jersey, more farmer than mechanic. He was looking at her curiously. 'Three miles beyond the village. Between the pine woods and the sea. Keep on this road another mile. Then take the fork to the right and you'll come to it. It's the only house on that road.'

The last house of the village stood at the crossroads. When she turned off the highway another car passed her, swinging out of the side road as she entered it. She caught a flash of its rain-spattered windshield and a placard that read *taxi*. Then it was gone toward the village, its lights and the light of the highway rolling away behind her. Now she was on a rough, winding track, hardly more than a trail with no light but her own headlamps to guide her. The little woods walled her in on both sides. Pine needles covered the ground, smothering undergrowth, leaving the slender tree trunks sheer as organ pipes with the wind singing through them. Already she could hear the deep mutter of the surf, like the purr of a good-humoured lion. She might have been a thousand miles from New York.

The trail dipped suddenly as she rounded a curve. Her headlights picked out a woman alone, walking blindly into the glare on the left side of the road. A tall, slim figure in dark hat and light coat – a long, black shadow that dwindled with sickening rapidity as the car shot forward.

Gisela stamped on the brake. The tyres lost traction. Like something in a dizzy nightmare, she felt the car lurch and skid out of control. She freed the brake and fought the wheel, which seemed to have a crazy will of its own. The car slewed around in a complete half-circle. Headlights raked the wall of pine trees and swept over a startled face, white as the dead, blotted out by an arm thrown up in self-protection. It was instantaneous and indelible as something seen in a flash of lightning: the parted lips, the stricken eyes that looked directly into hers. Then the car shuddered to a stop and the headlights went out.

Gisela sat still, trembling. After a moment, she found her voice. 'Faustina. Are you hurt?'

No answer. She tried to turn on the headlights. They no longer responded to the switch. She groped for a possible flashlight in the glove compartment. There was one. It worked. She crawled out of the car and turned the little spotlight on the road, dreading what she was about to see. But there was no one in sight.

'Faustina! Where are you?'

Again no answer – no sounds at all but the song of the wind, the whisper of the rain, the mutter of the surf.

Yet she had seen Faustina's face in that dreadful instant before the headlights went out. She had seen Faustina's blue covert coat and brown felt hat. Was Faustina knocked off the road by that shuddering impact? Lying in a ditch, unconscious or dead?

Gisela turned the flashlight down, moving its spot of light slowly over the roadway around the car. This dip in the road formed a muddy hollow. Already the rain was washing away the tracks her tyres had printed in the wet clay. There were no other tracks now – no footprints at all.

She climbed the shoulder of the road, turned her flashlight on the pine needles below. They glistened brown in the rain. They were close-packed, solid, slippery as ice. Apparently they had lain there undisturbed for years.

She no longer called Faustina's name aloud. She did walk several feet in either direction along both sides of the road. Still, there was nothing. No mark in the mud. No sign of blood. No dropped glove or wrenched heel – nothing.

She was wet and chilled to the bone when she climbed back into the car. She turned the ignition key and stepped on the starter. The engine kept silent, as if it were afraid to make a sound. *Short circuit*, she thought numbly. *That's why the lights went out.* In the dark, she groped for a cigarette, lit it with a match. For the first time in her life the taste of tobacco-smoke seemed nauseating. That was how she first realized that the chill she felt was not wind or rain alone, but fear.

She picked up the flashlight again and her purse. She got out of the car. It would be a longer walk back to the village than to Faustina's house. But the village was what she wanted now, with its lights and people and telephones. Only the slewing around of the car had confused her. The pine woods looked the same in either direction and the tracks that might have guided her were dissolved in mud. She started walking without any idea which way her steps would lead her.

After about ten minutes she realized that the surf was getting louder. She turned on the flashlight again. Underfoot, mud was giving way to beach sand and the woods were thinner here. Through tree trunks, she could see another light. She walked toward it.

Now the woods ended and she was passing between two high dunes crested with poverty grass. The light came from a house that stood on another dune at a little distance. She could hear the ocean loud and near, but where it must have been there was only a black void of starless sky and invisible water.

For a moment, she hesitated. Then she started down the sandy track toward the house.

The light coming from its front porch showed her a white picket fence around a garden of wild rose, bayberry, and Russian olive. She passed through a wide gate, walked up another sandy track. The house was built of unpainted shingles, polished pewter-grey by a bleaching sun and a scouring wind, laden with sand and salt water. Shutters and trim were painted white – a demure house, rather like a little old woman in silver taffeta and white kid gloves. Gisela's steps faltered. The light shining across the dunes actually came from the hall inside the house. The front door was open, swinging idly on its hinges with a faint jingle of metal that came from keys on a ring dangling from a latchkey in the lock.

On the threshold, she halted again and called out urgently: 'Faustina?'

Still no answer. She took a step into the hall and paused.

A single electric lamp burned brightly through a shade of white satin stretched taut over a metal frame. It stood on a telephone table in the curve of the stair, its tempered, domestic radiance spilling over white woodwork and white wallpaper flecked with green leaves. There was no other light.

The sound of ticking drew Gisela's glance to an old banjo clock, hanging on the wall opposite the front door. Its hands read twenty minutes after eleven. Beside it, the stair arched with the spirited trajectory of a waterfall, all white with moss-green carpet following its extended curve from step to step. At the foot of the stairs stood two small, shabby suitcases – the two Faustina had taken with her when she left Brereton.

Slowly, Gisela moved toward the only other opening in the hall – an archway on her right. Through it she saw two living-rooms divided by double doors made like french windows – glass panes set in narrow wooden frames. The first room was lighted indirectly by the light from the hall lamp. The other room, farther from the archway, was dusky with shadows, dim and confusing.

Once again Gisela raised her voice. 'Faustina! It's I, Gisela. Where are you?'

This time the silence seemed almost unbearable.

Deliberately, Gisela made a clatter as she set purse and flash-light down on a small table in the first living-room. Her glance travelled around the room, searching for a light switch, and found one in the wall, on the other side of the table. She was skirting the table, her hand already raised toward the switch, when her feet struck against something soft and resistant. She looked down. Breath fled her throat in a hoarse gasp.

Faustina Crayle was lying on the floor, face down, as if she had fallen facing the farther room. She was still wearing her blue covert coat, but her brown felt hat had rolled beyond her head. Her left hand, curled beside her shoulder, was covered with a brown leather glove. Her right arm stretched beyond her head, as if she had tried to ward off a blow. Her right hand was bare. A crumpled glove lay beside it and a handbag, its frame gaping open, scattering the vain trivia of powder, lipstick, and coin purse across the floor. Nowhere on her clothes or her person was there a splash of mud, a spot of dampness. Even her stockings and the soles of her shoes were dry and clean.

Her face was hidden by the veil of fine, pale hair tumbled across it. Gisela knelt beside her.

'Faustina! Are you hurt? Did the car strike you?' Gisela's fumbling fingers could find no pulse in the cold flesh. But that meant nothing. In first-aid classes during the war, she always had trouble finding her own pulse.

Gently, she pushed the hair away from the face. That face had always been pale, the lips often relaxed and parted as they were now. The thing that frightened Gisela was the eyes. Lids open, pupils dilated, they looked so blank. As Gisela turned the head toward the light, the lids did not flicker, the pupils did not contract.

Only then did she finally believe that Faustina was dead. Yet there was no bruise or cut in her flesh. No bullet hole in her clothing, no knife slit. There was not even a drop of blood.

Gisela sprang to her feet and pushed the light switch. But no light came. She looked up at the globe of ground glass in the ceiling, then down at the switch itself. It was the sort that is pushed up or down. Now it was down and the letters on this side were: ON.

She looked slowly around the room, as if she were trying to question those walls that must have seen whatever happened such a short time ago. The lamp in the hall burned steadily and its light, filtering through the archway, showed her more green and white wallpaper, and a rose-patterned chintz. She could hear the rhythmic crash and retreat of the surf – nothing else, not even the beating of her own heart, that felt as if it must be thudding aloud. She was almost certain she was alone in the house, but she could not be sure. She ran toward the telephone in the hall.

CHAPTER FOURTEEN

So rang, thrown down, the Devil's die
That won Faustine.

The radium-painted hands of the clock on the chiffonier pointed to 2.57 when the telephone pealed beside Basil's bed. It was still dark outside the windows, but there was a dawn freshness in the air. Eyes sticky with sleep, he groped for the telephone; his response, a reflex: 'Hello?'

'Basil?'

The low, tremulous voice roused him instantly and completely as a splash of cold water.

'Gisela! Where are you?'

'In New Jersey. At Brightsea. Something dreadful has happened.'

'What is it?' He didn't have to ask. He knew. Only one thing could explain her calling him at this hour. Yet, when her voice put it into words, it seemed unreal. She spoke quietly:

'Faustina Crayle is dead.'

'Is that why you're there?'

'No. After I left you I – had time on my hands. I remembered Faustina's asking me to come down any time I was free, so – I did. She was dead when I got here. Heart failure. I called the police first, but they don't seem to believe my story. They were rather unpleasant, but – they did let me telephone you.'

'Who's in charge? State Police?'

'Yes. A Lieutenant Sears.'

'Let me talk to him. Then I'll get down to Brightsea as fast as I can. Keep your nerve and don't answer any more questions until I get there. Where will I find you?'

'At Faustina's cottage. Basil, I . . . Oh, here's Lieutenant Sears.' The voice that came over the wire was truculent. 'Now this happened in New Jersey – not in New York. See? The young lady says you're a friend who'll get her a lawyer. O. K. So I let her call you. But it has nothing to do with the district attorney's office in New York. See?'

Basil saw. He summoned every resource of tact. But when he put down the telephone he realized that tact was not enough. He switched on the bedside lamp and put through a call to the Flatbush home of his old friend, Assistant Chief Inspector Foyle, of the New York Police Department.

The Inspector answered with a drowsy oath. 'Can't you boys ever let me sleep for ten minutes? What in hell do you want this time?'

Basil's voice and Gisela's name changed his attitude. He had known them both when they first met in 1940. 'Sorry, Doc. I thought it was one of those guys in Centre Street. They still call the old man when they get in a jam. This Jersey thing is going to be tough. Those State cops are funny about their jurisdiction. I'll call a Captain of State Police there who happens to be a friend of mine and get him to call Sears. Anything I can do at this end?'

'There's a lawyer in New York named Septimus Watkins.'

'Sure, and there's a Statue of Liberty. I've known both all my life.'

'See if you can get him to name the people who will receive

the jewels that belonged to Faustina Crayle's mother, now that Faustina herself has died before her thirtieth birthday. Watkins himself is the legal heir, but he has private instructions to turn the jewels over to certain people without publicity.'

'What was the mother's name? Crayle?'

'Yes, but I have reason to believe that she was known professionally as Rosa Diamond.'

Foyle whistled softly. 'She was in the same class as Cora Pearl! Lord, I don't like to think how many years ago . . .'

'Was Rosa Diamond co-respondent in a celebrated divorce case in 1912?'

'She could have been. I don't recall.'

'I'm pretty sure she was. And I want the name of the respondent . . .'

The rain had stopped when Basil drove through Hoboken. The sun was rising when his car entered Brightsea. In that clear light, it had the look of dazzling cleanliness common to fishing villages, the barren sand being so much cleaner than the fertile loam of farming country. As he passed the filling station, he recognized a familiar figure. He pulled over to the kerb. 'Mrs Lightfoot?'

She had been talking to the mechanic. Now she turned in amazement. 'Dr Willing!'

Even at that hour she was exquisitely coiffed and dressed. She still had her air of serene authority. But something else was gone. Some inner strength of soul that had sustained her until now. It was like finding a handsome seashell, all sunset colours, brilliant glaze, intricate convolutions, then looking inside and finding the dead creature that had once made that shell for its home, now a dark, brittle thing, like a dried bean, rattling around in splendid emptiness.

'The New Jersey police called me last night,' she explained. 'I came by train, and I can't get a car to drive me to Miss Crayle's cottage.'

The garage man had not missed a word. 'Listen, lady, I told you I only got one driver and he's up at the cottage now, being questioned, because he drove Miss Crayle from the train last night. There's nobody left here but me, and I can't leave the filling station alone.'

'I should be most happy to drive you there,' Basil told Mrs Lightfoot.

'You're very kind. I must go. I feel responsible for poor Miss Crayle. Dr Willing, was it suicide? If I had not turned her out ...'

The garage man did not miss this, either. 'Just heart failure, the cops told me. Everybody around here knew Miss Crayle had a weak heart.'

'How do we get there?' asked Basil.

'Straight down that road and right at the crossing. Then on to the beach.'

They drove through the village and it seemed to sparkle in the early sunshine, fresh as a new-washed face after the wet night. The car swerved right into the little forest of Christmas trees, dipped into the hollow, still muddy, and rose again to the sandy track where the slender trees were more thinly scattered. Here their massed verticals were slashed by one low, endless horizontal, drawn exactly as a knife edge, where the blue sky met the bluer sea.

The car sped between dunes and came out on to the wide

beach. Basil looked at the grey cottage built against the highest dune and thought of that Edwardian magnate who had hidden Rosa Diamond away in this desolate spot. A change from Paris, yet – if Rosa had any spark of poetry in her nature – she must have loved the sea and wind, the silence and solitude. She would not be lonely. To live alone or with one chosen lover is the courtesan's ideal of luxury.

Half a dozen cars were parked around the white picket fence. Basil found a vacant spot and shut off his engine. A man, whose full-blooded body seemed to strain the seams of his gaudy uniform, lounged forward.

'What do you want?' he demanded with the lack of grace the ignorant confuse with democracy.

'I have come to see Lieutenant Sears. My name is Willing.'

'Who's your girl friend?'

'Mrs Lightfoot is Miss von Hohenems' employer.'

'The Loot's busy. Why do you wanna see him?'

'Suppose you ask him that. He expects me.'

Basil's tone brought a dark flush to the trooper's face. 'Now, listen, you . . .'

The door of the house flew open and a voice called, 'Dobson!'

'Yessir?'

'Is that Dr Willing? Tell him to come in.'

'O. K.' Dobson turned back to Mrs Lightfoot and Basil. 'You heard the Loot. Get going.'

On the path, Mrs Lightfoot spoke in a dazed voice to Basil. 'Isn't there something like this in *Alice*? A footman who was a fish and insulted everybody at the door?'

Basil glanced back over his shoulder. Trooper Dobson was

eyeing them, legs straddling, arms akimbo. His eyes were puzzled and his lips moved silently, shaping the words: *A footman who was a fish* . . . ? What the . . . ?

In the open doorway stood a swarthy man, rather short for the physical requirements of a policeman, yet wearing the uniform of a lieutenant.

'Sorry about Dobson,' he said solemnly. 'Bone from the neck up and too big for his boots. I'm talking to reporters now. Please wait here in the hall for a few minutes.'

'And Miss von Hohenems?' asked Basil.

'She's O. K. Be right with you.' He darted through the archway into the living-room. 'Now, boys, right over here and make it snappy . . .' His voice receded to a murmur.

Mrs Lightfoot looked at the green-and-white hallway with approval. 'Like a little jewel box,' she said to Basil. 'Or a doll's house. Perfection in miniature.'

'Do you know who lived here before Miss Crayle?' asked Basil.

'No. Do you?'

'A woman named Rosa Diamond.'

'Oh!' Mrs Lightfoot turned startled eyes to him. 'Dr Willing, you have taken me back a thousand years! I didn't know that anyone of your generation had ever heard of Rosa Diamond. I only heard of her when I was a girl.'

'Did you ever hear the name of the man who brought her back to New York from Paris?'

Mrs Lightfoot was looking at the hall again, with greater interest. 'No,' she answered. 'I heard there was such a man, but I never heard his name. When she left Paris, she disappeared from public view.'

'I believe he was a New Yorker,' added Basil. 'He got a divorce and his wife named Rosa Diamond as co-respondent. Does that help your memory?'

Mrs Lightfoot shook her head. 'I'm sorry. You see I was really young at the time. I wasn't supposed to know there were such women.'

Sears appeared in the archway with two rather shabby young men. 'O. K., boys. That's it.'

'Thanks, Lieutenant.' They looked shrewdly at Mrs Lightfoot and Basil before they passed through the front door.

'Come in, please.' Sears made a motion toward the archway.

The glass doors were wide open now, the two rooms gay with sunshine, for there were bay windows in each facing one another.

Basil forgot Sears and Mrs Lightfoot as he saw Gisela's face haggard in the sunshine. In three strides he crossed the room, took her hands in his. They were cold to his touch, but she managed a weary smile. He pressed her hands, then turned to face Sears, 'Well? Why are you holding her?' He might have been the policeman and Sears a criminal.

Foyle must have done his best, for Sears answered, mildly enough: 'Where do you get the idea I'm holding her? She's free to go whenever she likes, only . . .'

'Only what?'

'If she'd just tell us a story that I could make sense out of there wouldn't be any "case" at all. She and this guy.'

Basil had not noticed the man. A small man with tousled hair, huddled in the corner of a sofa, wearing an old Army overcoat without insignia over a civilian suit. His eyes were harassed.

'But I told you three times, Lieutenant,' he whimpered. 'It was just like I said, honest to God!'

'Suppose you tell it a fourth time. This is Dr Willing from New York. Works in the district attorney's office there. Captain Lederer, my chief, called up and said I was to give him all information available. Information! There isn't any. You tell him.'

Quietly, Mrs Lightfoot found a chair near Gisela and smiled at her encouragingly.

The motion drew Sears's glance. 'I suppose you're Mrs Lightfoot, Miss Crayle's employer?'

'I was her employer until recently.'

'Why did she leave your school in the middle of a term? Miss von Hohenems won't tell us.'

Mrs Lightfoot answered carefully. 'Miss Crayle knew her subjects – the fine arts and draughtsmanship – but she didn't inspire the proper respect in her pupils.'

'Why not?'

'Lack of character, Mr Sears. You must find that important in your own field.'

'Sometimes.' Sears sounded dubious. 'O. K., Ronson. Go ahead.'

Basil, standing between Gisela and Mrs Lightfoot, heard the almost inaudible sigh of relief that escaped Mrs Lightfoot. She leaned her head against the back of her chair and half-closed her eyes in utter weariness. Once more she had kept Brereton out of the headlines.

They were sitting in the first of the two little parlours that became one long room when the dividing doors were thrown open, as they were now. The bay window at the far end of the second room framed a view of plunging surf, the gay blue and white of a della Robbia plaque. The two rooms were furnished almost exactly alike – frilled white curtains, white-shaded lamps, old-fashioned mahogany bookcases, rugs of faded rose colour the same shade as the roses on the chintz-covered sofas and armchairs. Hadn't the furnishings been changed since the rooms were first prepared for Rosa Diamond? Probably not. The pair of carved teakwood taborets with inlaid tops of pink marble, mottled as sausage, belonged to her period. Flowered chintz was a new fashion then, just imported from England. It must be she who had furnished the two rooms in the same colours so they would look like one long room when the dividing doors were thrown open. Perhaps it was she who had put in those dividing doors so the little fireplace would have a smaller room to warm on autumn days. There were no radiators. Of course, there wouldn't be in an old summer cottage like this. Was it she who had the doors made like french windows, so that when they were shut she could look through them to the bay window at the far end of the second room and its view of the sea?

All this brought Rosa Diamond suddenly to a brief life again, in Basil's mind. Richly red hair, swept up from the ears in the coiffure of the period: the long, narrow slit skirt that had just replaced the bell-shaped skirt of a few years before. In summer it would be thin stuff – grey or white or green or pale blue – no one would dare wear any other colours with red hair in 1912. And what had Faustina said? A long-handled sunshade of embroidered white linen. In winter she would wear sealskin. Mink was despised then as a poor imitation of sable. And she'd have a black hat with the uncurled ostrich feathers that were called *retour d'Auteuil* because women returning from the races in open carriages were once caught in a summer rain . . .

Rosa was intensely real to him for those few moments – a

slender figure with flaming hair standing in this very room beside a bay window open to the sun-warmed salt breeze of summer . . . or pouring tea before a cheerful blaze of driftwood on this hearth in the early dark of an autumn evening. And beside her, bending over her to breathe the fragrance of her hair and brush it with his lips . . . No. There the evocation failed. The unnamed man who had been Rosa's last lover and Faustina's father remained a shadow, almost a blank . . . Had she ever had regrets? Not the woman Basil saw so vividly in his mind's eye. She would smile and quote Marvel:

> *The grave's a fine and private place,*
> *But none, I think, do there embrace . . .*

All this flashed through his mind with a speed far greater than the velocity of sound or light – the speed of time itself. The man in the Army overcoat had just begun to speak: '. . . Miss Crayle took my taxi when she got off the ten-forty last night. It was raining cats and dogs, so I was at the station on the chance of picking up a passenger even though it's out of season now. I drove her right up to the porch steps here so she wouldn't get wet. I even carried her bags up on the porch for her, though she had only given me a ten-cent tip. When I got back in the car, she was on the porch, fitting her latchkey into the lock. I started the engine and I looked back over my shoulder to see if I had room for a half-turn without running into any of her rosebushes. I saw her then. She had left the front door open and she was just lighting a lamp in the hall here. I saw her bags in the hall and her key ring dangling from the lock in the front door. The last I saw of her she was standing beside the lamp she had switched on and there was a clock on the wall above her head that said eleven-five, just like the clock on my dashboard. Then I managed to make that turn, though it was a tight squeeze, and I ploughed through the wet sand to the road. When I reached the crossroads, another car passed me going toward Miss Crayle's house. It was eleven-twenty-five when I got back to the garage. And that's all I know.'

Basil looked at Sears. 'What's wrong with that?'

'The car he passed was Miss von Hohenems'. She remembers passing a taxi at the crossroads. When she got here the front door was still standing open with the key in the lock. The lamp lighted in the hall and the clock said eleven-twenty. The suitcases were right by that archway. Miss Crayle was in this room, lying on the floor, close to the light switch, and she was dead. Our doctor says there's no sign of violence on her body – just a diseased heart that happened to give up and stop beating as Miss Crayle reached for the light switch in this room a minute or so after Ronson here left her.'

'I still don't see what's wrong,' replied Basil. 'The two stories – Miss von Hohenems' and this man's – seem to agree in every detail. It's easy to reconstruct the rest – Miss Crayle did what most women do coming into a dark, empty house alone at night. She left everything – her key in the lock, her bag in the hall – until she could turn on a few lights. Unhappily she died alone in the dark before she had turned on any but the light in the hall.'

'O. K., let's take it a little more slowly,' responded Sears. 'She came straight into this room from the hall. She didn't stop to do anything else. She didn't take off her hat or coat or anything but one glove. She dropped her bags in the hall. She didn't even stop to close the front door or bring her key inside. How long would that take her? To walk from that table in the hall to this light switch in this room?'

'Less than a minute, I suppose.'

'Right. Then she must have died while Ronson was driving down the track to the pine woods, while he was still in sight of the house. He says he was going thirty, so it would take him eight minutes to reach the crossroads where he passed Miss von Hohenems' car. So Miss von Hohenems passed him at the cross-roads at eleven-thirteen. And Miss Crayle must have been dead by eleven-thirteen – right?'

'Dead or dying,' admitted Basil. 'Obviously she must have fallen just after Ronson left her at eleven-five, since she didn't have time to switch this light on.'

'She just had time for that,' amended Sears. 'The switch was on, but not the light, because both bulbs in the ceiling fixture are dead. How long would it take her to snap down that switch? A few seconds?'

'No more. What of it?'

'Merely this.' Sears leaned forward, his eyes intent and angry. 'Miss von Hohenems says that when she went through the pine woods after eleven-thirteen her car almost ran down a woman walking alone in the rain and she recognized that woman as her friend, Miss Crayle, who was at this house dead or prostrate and dying at least seven minutes before then. How could Miss Crayle be half a mile down the road, walking away from her house at that moment unless – one of these two witnesses is lying? And which one is it? Ronson? Or Miss von Hohenems?'

There was a gasp and a tinkle of broken glass on the hardwood floor. Mrs Lightfoot looked down wonderingly at her gloved hand. 'I was holding my pince-nez,' she said, slowly. 'I seem to have crushed the lens.'

CHAPTER FIFTEEN

The threads were wet with wine and all
Were smooth to spin . . .

Basil's car shot up the hill into the fairy-tale pine woods. The sweet spice of balsam was all around them, brought out by the warmth of the morning sun. On the crest above the hollow, he slowed to a full stop.

'Is this where it happened?'

'Yes.' Gisela, beside him, looked down into the hollow where wet clay had collected during the storm. Now it was beginning to dry, the surface a smooth crust, rayed with cracks. Beyond, the road swerved to the left, walled by a crescent of pine trees, strictly aligned as a file of soldiers at attention. A gull flew above the trees, shrieking for joy in the sun. The sound of surf reached their ears as a steady pounding – the lion, no longer playful, roaring deep in his throat.

'Any defence lawyer would make hash of an identification based on one glimpse in the headlights of a car,' said Basil. 'Sears knows that.'

'It was Faustina.' Gisela pushed back her dark hair from white temples marbled with blue veins and held her fingertips there, as if to still the throbbing of a headache. 'I saw her face, her eyes, as clearly as I see yours now.'

'But only for a moment,' Basil reminded her.

'I felt the shock to the car as it struck her and then – there was nothing there.' Her hands dropped to her lap. She closed her eyes and leaned her head against the back of the seat while the wind played gently with her hair.

'Faustina died – of heart failure,' she went on. 'Before you came Lieutenant Sears remarked that it was unfortunate her collapse came at that time when there was no one to help her. He even said she might have been saved if there had been someone with her to call a doctor . . . Don't you think there must have been some reason for her to die at that particular time? Even people with diseased hearts don't just fall down dead for no reason at all, do they? Not unless there is some little extra strain or shock to put a heavier load on the heart at that moment?'

'She carried her bags from the porch to the hall,' said Basil.

'But they weren't heavy.'

'She was tired after her journey and all the worries of the last few days.'

'I wonder.' Gisela opened her eyes without lifting her head and gazed into the infinity of blue above the trees. 'Doesn't modern medicine teach that physical death is a slow process, not the sudden act it appears in the eyes of the law?'

'Legal death occurs when heart and breathing stop,' answered Basil. 'But *rigor mortis* has been called "the death struggle of muscle". It's part of dying that occurs after heart and breathing have stopped. During the war Russian physiologists claimed they had revived soldiers an hour after they were legally dead by reanimating the heart.'

'You see? Legal death is a fiction. The elaborate ceremony of burial has blinded civilized people to the fact that dying is a long, slow process in the natural state. Perhaps what we call "dying" blends indiscernibly into the processes of decay and no one is really "dead" until the body itself is gone. Lawyers and coroners may say such-and-such a moment is the actual "moment of death", but it really isn't a momentary thing at all. It's a gradual disintegration of the organizing force that holds the body to a given rate of growth and temperature and keeps it functioning as a personality. The last breath is not the end of living, but the beginning of dying, a process that doesn't end until the body has rotted away.'

'Are you suggesting that Faustina died slowly? So slowly she was able to walk down the road and then back to the house again before she finally collapsed?'

'No.' Gisela extended a slim foot elegantly shod in brown alligator, but caked with mud. 'There was no mud on her shoes. They were dry and clean. Not even a splash of rain on her stockings.'

'What then?'

'If real death is a slow disintegration – and if there can be an immaterial appearance of a living person – could that appearance survive the legal death of the material body for a few moments? Especially if that death was sudden, violent stoppage of heart and breath, not real death at all?'

Basil smiled. 'Now we've come to it. The origin of all ghost stories.'

'What do you mean?'

'Historically, the idea of a double of the living seems to precede the idea of a double of the dead. Most anthropologists believe the double idea originated in the images of ourselves and others that we see in dreams. Once the primitive Egyptian or Greek had come to believe in the *ka* or *eidolon*, the next step was to wonder if this immaterial appearance always died with the death of the body? Or if it might not live on by itself? So was born that fear of the ghost which made Romans speak nothing but good of the dead, and which was gradually transmuted by time and the flux of ideas into a hope of immortality.'

'I wish we could establish the exact moment when Faustina's heart stopped beating.'

'Why?'

'Because I wonder if that was precisely the same moment when I felt the shuddering impact of my car and – the lights went out.'

Basil turned to look at her, astonished. 'You don't mean . . . ?'

'I can't help wondering – did the real Faustina die of shock at the very moment this wandering image of Faustina was struck by my car? Was it shock to the shadow that killed the substance?'

Basil shook his head. 'This is an extraordinary conversation for two reasonably mature and sophisticated people living in the twentieth century. It's an echo of half the myths in *The Golden Bough*. The old totemistic myth of the maiden who dies when the willow tree is cut down and the man who appears with his right hand missing after a hunter has cut off the paw of a wolf. Primitive man believed the double could enter an animal or a plant or even a stone, that it would suffer or die if its temporary home was destroyed.'

Gisela turned her head to look at him, smiling a little at her own fancies. 'I saw the figure in the road. You didn't. That's why I can never make you understand how real it was. Have you any explanation of your own?'

'Not yet. But there are several more things I'd like to know.'

'For instance?'

'Why did Faustina come down to this cottage at all at the present time? I advised her strongly to stay in New York for the next few days. I thought she intended to take my advice.'

'When she talked to me on the telephone she said something about meeting someone here this week-end – someone she wanted me to meet, too. I wasn't sure whether I could come or not.'

'So she came alone . . .' Basil added thoughtfully. 'And – death was waiting for her.'

'Death was waiting . . .' Gisela repeated the words slowly. 'But in what form? How could that be?'

'I don't know.' He looked at her haggard face and dark-lidded eyes. 'I'm going to drive you to the village inn and prescribe a sleeping pill. I'll call for you at dinnertime . . .'

The restaurant was in an attractive white frame house standing on a little rise of ground in a tree-shaded garden. A cheerful light shone through the dusk from a glass-enclosed porch where there were tables shining with glass and silver.

Gisela drew a deep breath of the clean country air and sighed. 'It's hard to believe this is the same world I was in last night – all rain and mud and darkness, and Faustina's body lying so horribly still on the floor.'

Basil was studying the wine list. 'I'm going to order a white Burgundy. If it's good at all, it will be very good. I want you to drink several glasses and forget all about last night.'

'What happened to Mrs Lightfoot while I was asleep?'

'She went back to Brereton. Sears promised her he would do what he could to keep all mention of the school out of the news-papers. That was what concerned her.'

'She can't be as coldblooded as all that. She did break those glasses, you know.'

'She was startled. So was I, at the time. But in ten days or so, she will have pushed all this out of her memory. People do that when a memory is unpleasant or inconvenient.'

'Was my car badly damaged? It was a borrowed car, you know.'

'A short circuit, as you thought. It's at the garage now. You can drive it back to Brereton tomorrow.'

'Why not tonight?'

'You're going to sleep again at the inn tonight. I settled that with Mrs Lightfoot. You had a bad shock and you must rest for another twenty-four hours.'

'But you . . .'

'I'm going to take a last look at Faustina's cottage now the police have gone. Sears gave me the key.'

A waiter brought the Burgundy, and Gisela took a sip. The sparkle came back into her eyes, a faint colour into her cheeks.

Basil put his hand over hers as it lay on the table. 'That's better.' For a moment he was completely happy and at peace.

But only for a moment. As the waiter left them a seedy young man sidled into his place.

'Miss von Hohenems?'

Gisela looked up and lost some of her new colour. 'Yes?'

'I represent the *New York Daily Reflector.* I wonder if you would care to give us a statement about your seeing Faustina Crayle on the road last night?'

Basil's hand closed tightly on Gisela's. His look should have withered the young man. 'Miss von Hohenems has no statement to make to the Press.'

'Who are you?' demanded the young man.

'My name is Willing.'

'Basil Willing? The psychiatrist in the DA's office?'

'Yes.'

'Are you a relation of Miss von Hohenems?'

'No. I'm engaged to marry her.'

'Oh . . .' The reporter was taken aback. But not for long. 'Is that for publication?'

'Certainly. But we have no other information to give you. Do I make myself clear?'

'Sure. Of course. Excuse me.' The young man hurried away. Basil heard him asking the first waiter he met for the nearest telephone.

Now Gisela's cheeks were a burning rose-red that made her eyes seem even darker and more brilliant. She spoke in a small, chastened voice. 'That was a very odd way to propose marriage.'

'Sorry. It seemed a good idea at the time – all things considered.'

'I really had no chance to say no, did I?'

'No. Do you want to?'

'No.'

'You mean – yes?'

'Yes.'

They laughed, enjoying the foolish confusion as if it were the most sparkling wit. They sat looking at each other, forgetting the wine and everything else.

Then an inner shadow clouded the light in Gisela's eyes. 'How did he know? Lieutenant Sears told me he wouldn't tell reporters.'

'Sears is not the only person who could have told. Some hint of your story must have leaked out, probably through one of the other policemen or the taxi-driver. The reporters put it up to Sears and he didn't dare deny it. He may even think the publicity will frighten you into revising your story. He probably thinks you imagined it. If you didn't, he probably wishes you would use your imagination now and retract it. For your story is the one thing that will make his report untidy. If you would only take it back, he could turn in a consistent account of natural death and forget the whole thing. We'll pick up some evening papers on our way back to the inn and see just how much he told reporters. Now let's try this French wine, which is probably Californian, with our English sole, which is probably the local flounder . . .'

They did not find a news-stand until they got back to the inn itself. There the only New York papers were the two tabloids whose flashy presentation of urban life is so dear to drab farming and fishing communities.

It could have been worse. One tabloid said Gisela was a beautiful Austrian countess. The other described her as one of the many greedy foreign refugees who were taking jobs away from red-blooded Americans. But both stories treated the incidents as a simple discrepancy – Gisela said she saw Faustina on the road after the time the taxi-driver claimed he had left Faustina at the house. Obviously neither Sears nor the tabloid reporters had heard the stories told about Faustina at Maidstone and Brereton. Basil shuddered a little as he thought of what the tabloids could do with that . . .

On his way to the cottage, he stopped at the garage to make sure Gisela's car would be ready in the morning. The lank countryman in jeans was leaning against a petrol pump, reading the worse of the two tabloids by the glare of an unshaded work-light.

'Car's O.K. now,' he announced, coming forward. 'Seen the evening paper?'

'Yes.'

'Funny.'

'Yes.'

He hesitated, pale-grey eyes searching Basil's face for some encouragement. 'Not the first time, you know.'

'What do you mean?'

'Well . . .' He looked down at a grease spot on the asphalt. 'Something odd about that Miss Crayle. One night this fall, I was out in my old heap and I saw her walking along a back road – alone. I stopped and offered her a lift. She just walked on without a word or a sound – as if she hadn't heard me. I was kind of sore. The old heap isn't much, but it still goes. So I just drove on. Then, a week later, she came down over Sunday. That was when she was teaching at some school in Connecticut. I saw her in the post office and I said something to her about this other time and she said I was mistaken. Said she hadn't been down here since last summer. Queer, wasn't it?'

'Yes.'

'Ever hear of anything like that before?'

'Not exactly.'

'My old grandmother is Highland Scot. She says things like that happen just before somebody is going to – pass away and now Miss Crayle has – gone.'

Basil noticed that the ancient taboo against speaking of death or evil by their right names was as strong as ever in this man. *Pass away – gone . . .* Could these transparent euphemisms make death more palatable to anyone? Aloud, he said, quietly: 'Better not tell any city reporters about it. They wouldn't believe you and they might make a funny story out of it. Bad publicity for your garage next summer, when the city people come here . . .'

Basil drove slowly as he came to the pine woods once more. The car dipped down into the hollow and rose on the other side without mishap. Tonight, even if headlights failed, no one could slip away through the woods unseen, for a thin new moon, sharp as a silver sickle, was shining through the tree trunks.

He came out of the woods, on to a scene of solitude and beauty. The white sand was silver in the moon's light. A few lines of surf glimmered almost as whitely along the edge of the sounding black void that was ocean. A breeze rustled in the Russian olives around the house, and the house itself was dark and quiet on its perch above the dunes. Perfect for a hermit or a poet or a pair of lovers.

Basil got out of his car and shut the door. The noise was loud in the empty stillness. Even his footfalls were magnified as he walked across the porch. He fitted the key in the lock. It turned easily and smoothly. He pushed the front door open and paused on the threshold, aware of the deeper silence indoors. He was sure that he was alone. There would have been some other quality in the silence if there had been anyone else there, living and breathing, however motionless.

He was standing where Faustina herself had stood only twenty-four hours ago. The storm was raging behind her, yet she had left the door open, the key ring dangling from the lock. Then she had crossed the hall and lighted the lamp on the telephone table. He did the same things. Now he could see exactly how much light came from the lamp after dark. It was as he had expected. Clear yellow radiance to the level of his waist. Above, shadows melting into darkness at the ceiling and the top of the stairs. He turned and walked through the archway as she had walked. His hand groped for the wall switch and found it, but he did not turn it on. He stood at arm's length from it and turned to face in the direction Faustina had been facing when she fell.

Again the light was about what he had expected it to be. A softened radiance in the first room, shadowy twilight in the room beyond. In that subdued light the white woodwork, the green-and-white wallpaper, and the rose-splashed chintz were cheerful and charming. Not a hint to warn her of the unexpected, the sinister . . . And yet – it was here that death was waiting . . . How? And why?

For several minutes he stood still, looking, thinking. The pretty room was like a bland, impersonal face that kept its own secrets. Was there one secret it could not keep?

At last he pressed the light switch. The white globe overhead blazed yellow, flooding the first room with brilliant light, leaving the further room in a paler radiance that was yet clear in every detail. Last night Sears had replaced the dead bulbs that baffled Gisela.

Basil walked about the two rooms, taking in detail. The place was well kept. Curtains freshly laundered, rugs and slipcovers clean, though faded by many washings. The white woodwork had the deep creamy glaze of wood that has been repainted many times, always by good professional painters. There was not a crack or a blister or a hair from the painter's brush anywhere on its enamelled surface. Only one flaw – a few scratches on the wooden frames that held the glass panes in the double doors between the two rooms. The scratches were so fine they might have been made by a sharp darning needle. They looked fresh.

Basil switched off the ceiling light and turned on a table lamp. There was firewood and kindling in a wicker basket beside the fireplace. He build a pyramid of wood and paper on the hearth, set fire to it, and pulled an armchair over to the blaze. He lit a cigarette and leaned back, his eyes on the crackling flames. Absorbed in thought, he hardly noticed when the fire began to burn low. The silence seemed deeper than ever now the crackling of the flames was gone . . .

He reached in his pocket for another cigarette. It was the last one in his case. He lit it and threw back his chin, exhaling smoke, his head tilted up against the high back of his chair. That posture brought his abstracted gaze to a mirror over the mantelpiece and its reflection of the archway into the hall. The burning cigarette fell from his hand, unnoticed.

How long had that silent figure been standing in the shadowy archway, its back to the hall? A tall, thin figure in a light coat. A dark hat brim shadowed a bloodless face. Pale, blurred eyes met his own gaze in the mirror – the eyes of a dead woman, Faustina Crayle. Since he could see those eyes in the mirror, they must be seeing him. He recalled his own naïve astonishment, long ago in childhood, when he was first told about that: if you can see someone else in a mirror, that other person can see you, even though you cannot see yourself there . . .

Was it only in the mirror? If he turned his head, would the archway be as empty as it was silent? Had he fallen half asleep as he mused before the fire?

The figure in the mirror moved. There was no sound behind Basil, but there was something else – a fleeting fragrance of lemon verbena.

Basil spoke, without moving. 'You had better come in . . .'

CHAPTER SIXTEEN

The games men play with Death
Where Death must win . . .

Now Basil rose to face the archway. His sudden motion created a slight draught. The dying fire flared up in a last bright flame. He went on speaking. 'The moment I noticed your family resemblance to Faustina Crayle, I knew you were the only person whom it was physically possible to mistake for her. You both had the ash-blond hair, the small head, and oval face with prominent nose and thin lips, the cloudy, blue eyes and the attenuated aristocratic figure – narrow flanks, fine wrists and ankles, slim hands and feet. She was tall for a woman, you are of medium height for a man. Your colour is higher, you do not walk or stand with her studiously stooped shoulders and your expression is bold and gay, while hers was mild and shy. But these are all superficial details that could be altered. Faustina's father died in 1922 and you were born in 1925, so it must be your grandfather who was Rosa Diamond's lover and Faustina Crayle's father. Faustina was your father's illegitimate half-sister, and your natural aunt. Still, I am not sure why you wanted her to die. Was it just to inherit the jewels your grandfather gave her mother? Or was it a morbidly romantic impulse to destroy the daughter of a woman who had wounded your grandmother's pride and taken jewels which you felt belonged to you?'

'Dr Willing, I give you my word I did not kill Faustina Crayle. I wasn't here when she died.'

'Can you prove that?'

'Of course not. An innocent man does not provide himself with an alibi. I spent a quiet evening at home – alone. But I know something of law – studied it for a year – and I know the mere absence of alibi never convicted anyone. To convict me you would need some witness to place me at the scene of the crime at or near the time it occurred. Can you do that? You may have some witnesses who saw or thought they saw Faustina Crayle or someone resembling her on the road. That is hardly the same as identifying Raymond Vining, is it? Not in a murder trial, where proof must be beyond all reasonable doubt . . .

'Another thing you'd have to connect with me is the means of death. From what I've heard from the police here, that would be impossible, too. There was no wound on her body. She died of heart failure. And – though I see you don't believe me – I truly was not present when she died.'

'I believe that last,' answered Basil quietly. 'She was alone when she died and yet – she was murdered.'

Vining was taken aback. 'You think that you know how she died?'

'I know that I know. And so do you.'

'Dr Willing, I wish you wouldn't take that tone with me. I have no idea how she died and – once you hear my side of the story you may understand why I am so utterly baffled by the whole thing. Perhaps you and I can put the pieces together between us and make out some dim outline of what really happened. I hope to God we can! Otherwise . . .'

'Otherwise what?'

'All the rest of my life I shall never know where reality ends and illusion begins. I shall be like a man walking on marshy ground, never sure whether the next step will land on solid earth or quicksand.'

Vining came out of the shadowy archway, into the middle of the room, and illusion died. By the light of the fire and the single lamp, he was a commonplace figure – a tall, slim, fair young man in a dark brown hat and a light overcoat of natural camel's hair. He tossed the hat aside, took off the coat, and pulled up a chair to the fire. He offered Basil a pack of cigarettes, virgin in cellophane. 'I saw you smoke your last one just now. I stood there some time before you noticed me in the mirror.'

'Why?'

'I was surprised. I wondered what you were doing here. When I saw the light, I thought the police had left a man on duty. Then I came to the archway and saw your face in the mirror.'

'I didn't hear a car.'

'I walked from the station. Couldn't find a taxi and I sold my own car a few days ago.'

'I didn't hear a step.'

Vining extended feet in beautiful brown calf, polished to the patina of old saddle leather. 'Crêpe rubber soles.'

'You have luxurious tastes. Yet you sold your car?'

'I'm hard up. Who isn't these days? My minimum for comfort is a thousand a month – twelve thousand a year. I make thirty-five hundred as a bond salesman, and I have an income of six thousand from stocks and bonds of my grandfather's, which have depreciated. It's not enough, but – I'm not starving.'

'The jewels he gave Rosa Diamond may have appreciated. You did know about them?'

'Oh, yes. Rosa told my grandfather her plan before he died. He told my father, who told me. I talked to Watkins this evening when I saw Faustina's death in the papers. Vining is one of six names on the list. I am to get a pair of ruby earrings worth about thirty thousand today and this cottage. Just before she died, Faustina made a will leaving the cottage to Watkins. He insists on turning it over to me because it was my grandfather's. It's too isolated for most people, so at the most it's only worth six or seven thousand. So I net about thirty-seven thousand out of Faustina's death. Even if I could have known the exact amount beforehand, do you seriously believe that I would plot to kill for that?'

Basil sighed. 'Men have been murdered for far less. And women.'

'Oh, I know men have been stabbed for fifty cents and children poisoned for a few thousand dollars' insurance. But not by sane men with an income of ninety-five hundred a year and a position in life to lose.'

'Thirty-seven thousand would mean a great deal to you now. And you must have hated Rosa Diamond's daughter.'

'I didn't. I'm not morbidly romantic. My grandfather only met Rosa Diamond after he had left my grandmother and it all happened long before I was born. I don't shock easily and I'm not the type to carry on a blood feud for three generations, am I? As a matter of fact, I've always thought the Rosa Diamond affair lent a certain dashing naughtiness to what was otherwise a very stuffy, respectable family. I'm rather proud of it.'

'Why did you come here tonight?'

'To look over the cottage, now it's mine. I can't get away from the office as often as I'd like by day.'

'When did you first meet Faustina Crayle and discover her resemblance to you?'

'If I were canny, I suppose I wouldn't tell you. But I'm going to risk it, because you may be able to explain the things I don't understand myself. No one else knew the truth, but Alice, and now – she's dead . . .'

Basil interrupted.

'For a long time, I've realized that Alice and Faustina were not the only connecting links between Maidstone and Brereton. You were a third link between the two schools because you were engaged to Alice a year ago when she was there.'

'That's how it all started.' Vining leaned forward, his eyes on the fire, his hands dangling between his knees. At last Basil could give form and substance to the figure that had stood beside Rosa Diamond in this very room so long ago – turning her music pages at the piano, drinking her tea before the fire. A slender, supple man whose crisp hair was edged with gilt in the firelight, whose blue eyes were like Faustina's and Meg's – misty bright as star sapphires, but, unlike theirs, alive with daring and mockery . . .

'Maidstone was strict,' began Vining. 'No male visitors except Sunday and then under supervision. That was a challenge to me. I used a trick as old as pagan Rome. Remember how the intrusion of young Clodius in woman's dress at a religious rite reserved for women caused Caesar to divorce the wife that wasn't above suspicion? Like Clodius, I was young, rather slight, and beardless. I knew I could pass as one girl among many if I wore a girl's hat and coat, stockings and shoes, and kept at a safe distance from others, in a dim light. Nearly every girl at Maidstone had a camel-hair coat, so that was simple. The hat brim shadowed my face, but, to make sure, I dusted my cheeks with white powder and under the hat I wore what women's hairdressers call a "transformation" of false hair the same colour as my own. I got in by a french window, slipped up the back stairs and met Alice on a balcony there, while everyone else was downstairs. It was fun, you know. Added the spice of conspiracy to what might have been otherwise a rather stupid little flirtation . . .

'The next Sunday when I met Alice officially, in my own clothes, she told me with great glee that I hadn't passed for just any girl among many – I had been mistaken for a particular girl, one of the young teachers, Faustina Crayle. Someone coming up the drive had seen me on the balcony and got into quite an argument with another girl who insisted that Faustina was in the library at that very time.

'I had never heard the name Faustina, but I knew that Rosa Diamond's real name was Rose Crayle and I knew there had been a daughter, whose name should have been Vining. So I suspected instantly why there was such a likeness between this Faustina Crayle and myself. I even told Alice about it.'

'And, having succeeded once by chance, you then took advantage of Faustina's resemblance deliberately and wore woman's dress whenever you visited Alice secretly at Maidstone? Six times altogether, wasn't it?'

'Now we've come to it.' Vining was still looking down into the fire. Its glow dusted the fair down of his cheek with a pollen of light. 'That's the whole point. That's the thing I can't explain. The thing you won't believe.'

'What is it?'

'It gives you a queer feeling when a joke turns into – something else. Two weeks later, Alice and I were both in New York for the Christmas holidays and I met her at a sub-deb dance. She was angry. Even now I remember her very words. She said: "So you did it again. You'd better be careful! Once is enough. If you keep it up you'll get caught and then we'll both be in trouble."

'I suppose I said something like: "What are you talking about?"'

'She went on: "Someone saw you at Maidstone last week, dressed as a girl again. I suppose you got cold feet before you got to my room and left without seeing me."

'I said: "Nonsense, I wasn't there at all. I wouldn't try a thing like that twice."

'To my amazement, she didn't believe me. There had been another argument between two girls, each claiming to have seen Faustina in different places at the same time. It was all so circumstantial, that Alice jumped to the conclusion I was visiting one of the other girls at Maidstone. It made her furiously jealous. That was the real reason we quarrelled and broke off our friendship.' Vining turned his pale eyes so like Faustina's in all but expression toward Basil. 'Dr Willing, on my word of honour, I only went to Maidstone in girl's dress once. I didn't dare risk it a second time. So – what really happened at Maidstone? What was it they saw?'

Basil studied the grave young face. 'I could say that your single appearance as Faustina started the thing and the rest was hysteria and malobservation, fanned by the books on psychic research Miss Maidstone kept in her study.'

'Then – what happened at Brereton?'

'I take it you're going to deny that, having discovered by accident you could impersonate Faustina at Maidstone, you deliberately planned to do so at Brereton?'

'Why, in God's name, should I do anything so futile and so foolish? I was an undergraduate at Harvard last year when I played that one silly trick at Maidstone. This year, I'm a man with a living to earn and a little sister to support. Why should I waste my time and attention on such a dreary, long-drawn, practical joke? Frightening little girls at school, including my own sister, and running poor Faustina out of a job she really needed? A joke I couldn't share with anyone else?'

'You could have shared it with Miss Aitchison.'

'Alice was not amused. As the thing snowballed, she was afraid the truth would come out about that first episode and we'd both suffer for it. She was particularly afraid Faustina herself would catch on. At Brereton, Alice tried to intimidate Faustina by making Faustina believe that she, herself, was playing psychopathic tricks unconsciously.

'The day of the school party at Brereton, I left early because Alice had asked me to meet her at the summerhouse in the garden at a certain time. We were pretty sure of being alone there. It was such a cold day people wouldn't go into the garden. And we were too far from the drawing-room windows to be overheard. Alice was in a flaming temper. She had asked me to meet her privately because she wanted to know why I was still impersonating Faustina Crayle. You see, she thought I was visiting some other girl at Brereton. She even tried to make *me* jealous by telling me she was going to marry Floyd Chase.'

'How did you answer her?'

'How could I answer her? The more I realized she was serious, the more unnerved I became. It was the first I had heard of the double appearing at Brereton. I couldn't argue with Alice – at last I just left her standing there alone beside the summerhouse and walked down the drive to my car and drove back to New York. Can you imagine how I felt? There's an old story of a charlatan medium – is it Browning's *Sludge*? Anyway, some fraud who faked ghostly rappings for his clients night after night and then, one night, before he had begun to fake, there came a rapping. Only he, of all those present, could ever know that one thing was genuine. The others had believed the whole thing genuine all along. So he couldn't tell them without giving himself away. If he had called in some sceptic as an independent witness – well, there was evidence of fraud all over the place. It must have – upset him, don't you think? To know something like that and not be able to confide in anyone? How frightened he must have been, deep down, inside, when he realized that there was – something he had mocked with his crude, commercialized imitation. Something that might even resent the mockery . . .

'Once, at Maidstone, I played one ridiculous undergraduate prank and all this other seems to have come out of that. But who would believe my story? It's so much more reasonable to assume that I'm a liar, that I've been doing the whole thing all along . . . I've thought of collective hallucination sparked by my one appearance as Faustina at Maidstone. I'd be glad if I could believe anything so sane and simple. But when I heard Meg's story and your account of Emilie Sagée, I thought of something else . . .

'It must have been a great shock to Faustina herself when she first heard the stories about that other Faustina at Maidstone, especially after she read Miss Maidstone's books. Could that shock have been a sort of catalyst, disintegrating her whole personality in some way we don't understand and so making the other appearance psychologically possible?'

Basil's response came slowly. 'Then how do you account for Faustina's death?'

'Heart failure means shock – fear. She came down here alone and saw something. Does any other explanation cover all the facts?'

'You really want me to tell you?' asked Basil.

'Indeed, yes. Any explanation would be better than this feeling of mystery and doubt.'

'Well,' Basil spoke judicially. 'Let's take it step by step: We'll assume you're telling the truth about your first escapade at Maidstone. You wore woman's dress in order to visit Alice when she was a pupil there. You were mistaken for Faustina. As she could not have been where you were seen at that time, some superstitious servant or some young girl brought up by a superstitious nurse, began to whisper the old legend of the fetch or *doppelgänger*. Insidiously, the hysteria permeated the whole school. Miss Maidstone herself was a dabbler in the esoteric, so she was psychologically unable to crush it as an unbeliever would have done.

'You learned all this from Alice. You recognized the name Crayle and realized that the resemblance came from a blood relationship. You knew from your father that you would inherit Rosa Diamond's ruby earrings if Faustina died before her thirtieth birthday and you knew what they were worth. You were stung by the irony of the fact that you, the legitimate heir, had inherited stocks and bonds that had depreciated while Faustina, the illegitimate heir, would inherit jewels that had appreciated. Your father may even have mentioned the fact that Faustina had inherited your grandfather's weak heart. You began to think with a certain pleasure of the possibility of Faustina's death. But you had no wish to be tried for murder and possibly convicted. It was then that you saw how you could use this chance crossing of your path and hers to murder her without even being suspected, if you had any luck at all.'

'Murder?' Vining's eyes widened blankly, almost innocently. 'That's a large word, Dr Willing. How do you think I did it when I wasn't here at the time?'

'You weren't here when Faustina died, but you may have made a special trip down here some weeks or months ago and looked through the windows when they were unshaded.'

'Why should I do that?'

'To verify the fact that the plan of the house and its furnishings had remained unaltered to this day. I realized they had as soon as I saw the faded chintz and the old-fashioned teakwood taborets. There are a hundred ways you could have known about the original furnishings – family traditions about the house, even group photographs showing the interior. After all, this house had been your grandfather's before he met Rosa Diamond.'

'But why should I care about the house plan and furnishing?'

Basil's gaze held the pale eyes. 'I'll tell you in a moment. So far my story has followed yours in regard to every fact, differing only in the interpretation of facts. But at this point we part company in regard to facts, too. For I say: you continued to appear in woman's dress at Maidstone so that the general belief in Faustina's double would be strengthened and word of it would ultimately reach Faustina herself. On these later occasions, you took pains to dress exactly like Faustina, you imitated her posture, her gait, and gestures, you even subdued your own rather impish expression to her look of wistful seriousness. You were silent as a phantom on rubber-soled shoes. You were careful to appear only in a dim light and at a safe distance from eye-witnesses. By this time you knew the Sagée story – you would look up the history of the *doppelgänger* – and you took pains to reproduce some of its most dramatic details. You could not take Alice Aitchison into your confidence. She was too flighty for an accomplice. She might have given you away at any moment. Perhaps you hoped she would come to believe in the double herself . . .

'You were delighted when Faustina was dismissed from Maidstone because of the double. Losing a job is a very real thing and the cause can never seem wholly unreal. Faustina herself would believe in the double now, and that was essential to your plan. You traced her to Brereton. Because she was there you sent your little sister to Brereton – Mrs Lightfoot told me the child had been going to a New York day school until this fall. But you had to know what was going on at Brereton and you knew Meg would act as an unconscious spy for you, so she was transferred there. Unfortunately for Alice Aitchison, she got herself a job at Brereton when she heard your sister was there, hoping it would bring her in touch with you again, for she was still in love with you.

'At Brereton you repeated your performance as Faustina's double, still using french windows for entrance and exit and a back stairway for inconspicuous transit. Faustina had changed her camel's-hair coat for blue covert. You bought one like it and copied her outdoor dress in every detail, so you always had an excuse for wearing a hat which would shadow your face. You chose your witnesses carefully – ignorant, suggestible maidservants and flighty little girls of thirteen or fourteen, one your own sister. As at Maidstone, you were careful to appear only at a safe distance from these eye-witnesses in a light that was dim and deceptive. But careful as you were, it was inevitable that your luck couldn't hold when you appeared so many times. Inevitably you made a few miscalculations and had several narrow escapes any one of which might have wrecked your whole plan if you hadn't kept your nerve. Once you had to lock the front door to delay Alice and Gisela whom you saw coming up the drive and give yourself time to leave the house by another route. Once you had to pass the maid, Arlene, on the back stairs, too close for comfort, but daylight was fading and you had the audacity to carry it off. On another occasion you were nearly trapped upstairs and so forced down the front stair past Mrs Lightfoot herself. You would not have chosen such a mature witness deliberately even at long range. At short range, it must have been a torturing experience for you. But you had the presence of mind to pass her swiftly, even rudely, counting on the suddenness of your passage to disconcert her, and you slipped out a french window in the dark drawing-room just as Arlene was entering the lighted dining-room, where she couldn't see you. The last two instances are the only occasions when you appeared close to any-one and I am convinced both were inadvertent on your part – two bits of bad luck. But once you had carried them off successfully they gave enormous verisimilitude to the story of the double. People would argue: surely a fraud would not take such risk of detection . . .

'There was always risk in all these appearances of yours but one thing protected you – superstitious fear kept the witness at a distance. And I believe your temperament enjoys risk as a stimulant.

Besides, up to this time, you had done nothing seriously criminal, although masquerading as a woman in public is technically an offence. If you were caught, it could be passed off as a practical joke – in shocking taste, no doubt, but still not a serious crime . . .

'Alice Aitchison's presence at Brereton was another irritating piece of ill luck – something you had not allowed for in your calculations. Of course the moment she heard the new stories about Faustina at Brereton she knew that you were the so-called "double". She couldn't guess your purpose and doubtless she assumed again that you were using your old trick to visit some other girl there. At first she still loved you enough to protect you by urging Gisela not to let me know what was happening there. But you understood that as soon as Alice realized she had lost your love beyond recall she would no longer protect you and she would probably betray you. The day of the school party she was already turning to another man, Floyd Chase. Then you knew that you would have to kill her.'

'Alice!' Vining appeared startled, and incredulous. 'You think I killed Alice?'

Basil's answer was matter-of-fact. 'You had to kill her because she was the only person in the world who knew you could impersonate Faustina successfully.'

'Why should I care?'

'Because that made Alice the only person in the world who would be able to guess just how you could kill Faustina without being present at the moment of her death. Alice had to die before Faustina or you would not be safe.

'You left the school party early – just after telling Gisela you were going to walk down the drive and sample the whisky in your car. Actually, you went back to your room at the village inn to get your copy of Faustina's blue coat and brown hat before you met Alice by appointment at the summerhouse. You had chosen that meeting-place because it was five hundred feet from the house. Anyone who happened to see you from a window at that distance would see you as Miss Crayle.

'You said a moment ago that you left Alice standing beside the summerhouse, alone. Beth Chase told a different story. She said: "Miss Crayle put out her hand and pushed Miss Aitchison and she screamed and fell backward down the steps." Did you strike Alice a blow that must break her neck? If so, it was an adroit piece of calculated daring. If you were seen at all you would be seen at a distance and identified as Faustina. If Faustina had no alibi she might be accused of murdering Alice. If Faustina did have an alibi, there would be whispers about the double again, with a long history to support that fantasy going all the way back to Maidstone and witnesses who had no motive for perjuring themselves. In that case the police would write the whole thing off as "hysteria", while Alice's death would greatly increase the fear most other people felt for the double – including Faustina's own fear of it.'

Vining had listened to this accusation with an impersonal interest that would have taxed the self-control of another man. But though his flesh looked fair and firm and blooming in the rosy light of the fire, there seemed to be something sickly at the core of the man – a curious emotional deadness as if the natural human responses were anaesthetized or atrophied.

At last he spoke, without apparent resentment. 'Now I know why they say circumstantial evidence is misleading,' he remarked as conversationally as if they had been discussing someone else.

'You've built up a beautifully consistent case against me. It's quite fascinating to see how each point falls into place – how all the right facts can be made to fit a wrong theory. But there's one thing more, the nub of the whole business. How did I kill Faustina? She did die a natural death, you know. Heart failure. And I wasn't here when she died. I swear that.'

'Of *course* you were not here when she died,' returned Basil. 'That would have spoiled everything.'

'How?'

'Let me quote her own words: "Suppose when I'm quite alone in my own room I should suddenly see a figure and face close to mine and recognize it as my own face in every detail and every flaw, even this pimple on my left cheek – then I'd know it was real and I believe I should die . . ."'

Vining's fingertips touched his smooth cheek. 'But I don't have pimples. And I wasn't here.'

'Did you ever enter a strange room by twilight and see a stranger coming toward you? And then realize, with a rude jar to your faith in your own sense of recognition, that the stranger was merely yourself, reflected in a mirror?'

'This room wasn't strange to Faustina,' retorted Vining. 'The only mirror is over the mantel, too high to be mistaken for reality.'

'You knew this house and these two parlours; you knew that they are exactly alike in size and shape, in number and position of windows, furnished in the same colours, with almost all the same things, and divided from each other only by double doors of – glass . . .

'Did you simply tack a black curtain behind the glass? Or did you fit a square of black cardboard behind each pane within its frame, the way amateur painters do when they are painting small window frames and don't want to smear the glass? There are scratches on the frames now. Perhaps afterward you had to pry the cardboard out hastily with a sharp needle . . . And, of course, you put dead bulbs in the ceiling fixture of this front parlour.

'Faustina let herself into the dark, empty cottage with a latchkey, leaving it in the door while she turned on the hall lamp. It was chance that she stepped into the front parlour the next moment. But she was bound to enter it sooner or later that evening and when she did – only one thing could happen. She would press the light switch just inside the hall archway. No light would come, since the bulbs were dead. A movement would draw her eyes to the glass doors – now a mirror with something black behind them. Whose movement? Her own, reflected there. But she wouldn't know it was a reflection. She would believe, with absolute conviction, that there was transparent glass in those doors. She knew nothing of a black backing. There was nothing to tell her that she was looking at a reflection of the front parlour in an improvised mirror instead of the second parlour viewed through glass, since both were so nearly alike. The low, irregular light that came from the single lamp in the hall would be deceptive by the time it reached the second parlour. It wouldn't show the side wall of that room which differed from the first room in one way – it had no fireplace.

'You see what happened? Faustina's own reflection killed her because she saw it where she believed no mirror could possibly be – in those doors she knew to be of glass. For over a year her mind had been subjected to intensive psychological preparation for belief in the myth of the *doppelgänger*. *She who sees her own double is about to die.* And she had a weak heart, so ... She toppled down, frightened to death by the oldest, the simplest of all illusions – her own reflection. She lay dead of terror when there was nothing to terrify anyone – merely glass, insensate and colourless as water, imaging the prone body of a dead girl.

'The cleverness of your method was its combined use of both impersonation and reflection. In Faustina's own mind her phantom double was invested with the properties of both and so could not be one or the other, but must be a true phantom. No reflection could move freely indoors and out where there was no glass, as you did at Brereton. No reflection could be seen simultaneously with Faustina herself, while she and it were performing different actions as occurred at Brereton. But while those things might suggest impersonation, no impersonator could reproduce Faustina's face and figure and clothes so exactly in every detail as the image she saw last night in your improvised mirror. Let her believe that the two phenomena were one and the same thing – and she was lost.'

'You're doing a wonderful job of imaginative creation, Dr Willing. Do tell me how I knew Faustina would come down to her cottage that particular evening?'

'You telephoned and asked her to meet you here. Someone did, you know. She mentioned it in veiled terms to Gisela, without identifying you by name. No doubt you introduced yourself as one of her father's mysterious family, which she had wondered about for so long. You could tell her things about Watkins and her mother that would identify you without mentioning your name. Perhaps you told her she was illegitimate, so she'd understand your wish to meet secretly and avoid scandal. It would be a powerful lure to a lonely girl like Faustina.'

'And while Faustina was dying, I suppose I was establishing an alibi?'

'No. That would be crude. You are subtle. And you had to remove the cardboard or curtain or whatever you used, before anyone found the body. So you came here just after Faustina died. Again you were dressed as Faustina Crayle, just as you were when you came to this village a few days before to turn the glass doors into a mirror and a garage man offered you a lift on the road. With luck, you might not have been seen either time. As it happened, you were seen both times and mistaken for Faustina, as you had planned. You knew that if the police discovered that Faustina was "seen" after she was dead only one thing could happen – the story of Faustina's double would become the story of Faustina's ghost and eventually the police would dismiss the whole matter as village superstition.

'Last night you removed the black cardboard a few minutes after Faustina died. You had every reason to believe you would be alone in the house for hours. But then you heard a car coming through the woods. Another piece of bad luck. Faustina had invited a week-end guest, Gisela. So you couldn't wait to replace the dead bulbs with live ones as you had intended. You had to make a dash for the woods, leaving the front door open and the hall lamp burning just as Faustina had left them. You tried to get through the trees without being seen, but it was a dark night and you stumbled on to the road where Gisela nearly ran over you in her car. When her headlights short-circuited, you got away silently on rubber soles. The slippery crust of pine needles took no footprints and the rain washed away the prints in the road before Gisela turned on her flashlight.'

'A magnificent piece of fiction, but – nothing more.' Vining laughed softly. 'You have no evidence.'

'Haven't I? There are a few points.'

'Such as?'

'Every living body has some odour – clothing, shaving lotion, something. Mrs Lightfoot was the only reliable witness close to the double at Brereton and she said it had none. Does that mean it was really inhuman? Or is there some condition that makes one body seem odourless to another? There is just one such condition: when two bodies have the same odour. Two women using the same perfume cannot detect it in one another. A non-smoker kissing a smoker is keenly aware of nicotine fumes, but two smokers, kissing each other, will each believe the other has a clean breath. Mrs Lightfoot uses lemon verbena. Since the double was odourless to her, it must be someone else who uses lemon verbena, too. Someone in whom it is such an ingrained habit that he forgot to suppress it when he was impersonating Faustina. Probably a man, since Mrs Lightfoot said the stuff she used was a man's lotion. Certainly not Faustina herself, since she used nothing but lavender.

'That narrowed my search for the double considerably. Some-one who looked enough like Faustina to pass for her at a distance in a dim light, someone who used lemon verbena habitually, some-one who had connexions with both Maidstone and Brereton, someone who had some motive for injuring or destroying Faustina.

'When I entered my library last night, I caught a hint of lemon verbena, but I wasn't sure which of you three it came from – Mrs Chase or Chase or you. Just now when you were standing in the archway, I caught that delicate fragrance again and I knew it came from you.'

Vining maintained his anaesthetic detachment. 'Neat. Ingenious. Plausible.' He spoke with intellectual enthusiasm. 'But, unfortunately, not true. I mean, the whole thing. Of course, I do use a *verveine* lotion after shaving ... But I've told you the truth about myself and Faustina. You may not believe it. But I know it's the truth, whether you believe it or not. And even if you do believe in your own conjectures you can't prove them. That lemon verbena business is too thin.'

He rose and strolled around the room restlessly, hands in pockets, looking at the glass doors and the overhead light fixture, apparently with the idle curiosity of a tourist regarding a place where history was made long ago. He paused and smiled, his puckish, daring smile. 'I've always said a successful murderer must know the law. That's his only chance.'

'What do you mean?'

'You know, of course. You must. Otherwise, we'd be in a police-station together instead of enjoying this delightful heart-to-heart talk, like the ending of a detective story. Even if everything you said was true – which I'm not admitting – I still wouldn't be a murderer.'

'Why not?'

'Ah, you think I don't know the answer. But I do! If I had killed Faustina the way you say, I should be thankful now for that year of law I took before I decided on bonds instead. As you very well know, my dear Dr Willing, it's practically impossible to prove murder or even homicide when you kill a person by frightening him to death. Especially if the victim is known to have a weak heart. How could you ever prove in court that anything I did caused the heart attack? She might have had it anyway for a hundred internal or external reasons. Legally and medically you can prove that a physical injury is the cause of death – a bullet wound, a knife cut, a blow, poison – but who can prove that a mental injury caused a heart attack – beyond all reasonable doubt? And that's what you have to prove to convict for murder or homicide. District attorneys don't prosecute cases they can't win. In a civil suit, you need only the preponderance of evidence to prove your case, so, in cases such as this – death by mental injury or shock – the worst that can happen to you is a civil suit for damages brought by the victim's family, but – poor Faustina had no family. She was a bastard.'

Basil rose. 'You've forgotten one thing: Alice Aitchison was not frightened to death. Beth Chase saw her pushed down that staircase by someone who looked like Faustina and wore Faustina's clothes. It can be proved that you bought clothes like Faustina's. It can be proved that you were Faustina's blood relative illegitimately, and that of all the people at Brereton that day you alone resembled her enough to be mistaken for her in clothes similar to hers. And it can be proved that you had quarrelled with Alice – for whatever reason. It is for Alice's death that you will be convicted, Vining. I'm taking you into custody now.'

For the first time, Vining surprised Basil. Calmly Vining said: 'As you please. I hardly care.'

'Why not?'

'Suppose I were acquitted. I should have to go on living with this.'

'Your guilt?'

'Nothing so simple. Just try supposing for the sake of argument that my story is true. Where does that leave me?' The pale, enigmatic eyes looked through the unshaded window at the prodigal glitter of stars spanning the sky from horizon to horizon. 'I know

I am innocent. I know I didn't carry out this elaborate hocus-pocus you describe, but – I'm the only one who can know that, so . . . I'm the the only one who has to face some rather uncomfortable questions. And I have to face them alone. What did happen at Maidstone and Brereton? And what was it Faustina saw when she entered this parlour last night and died of shock?'

'You persist in that fantasy? Even now?'

'Of course. There are some points you didn't cover. Why did Faustina herself move in such trancelike slow-motion all during the time Meg and Beth were seeing the – mirage of Faustina?'

'Faustina was taking vitamin pills with her meals. You had every opportunity to substitute pills the same size and colouring containing some mild soporific. That's why the vitamins didn't help Faustina's languor and anaemia, as Alice noticed. It was easy for you to time your appearances as the double so they occurred at the right interval after a meal, when the drug would begin to take effect on Faustina. When she left Brereton she would take the pills with her and that's why her voice sounded sleepy just after tea when she talked to Gisela by telephone during the school party. The whole thing was another detail you copied from the story of Emilie Sagée. She, too, moved drowsily when her double appeared.'

'You think you can explain everything, don't you? Then try explaining this: how could anyone like me, impersonating Faustina, know that Faustina had a repressed impulse to pass Mrs Lightfoot on the stair and carry out that unspoken impulse of Faustina's?'

'Chance. Your good luck. Faustina's bad luck.'

'Chance? Luck? Is that the best you can do? Whenever I think about that particular incident I feel – uneasy, don't you?'

He was so serious that, for a moment, Basil almost believed him. Then the overwhelming weight of a scientific education was thrown into the balance on the other side.

'Why bluff, Vining? There are no witnesses here tonight. I can never prove to anyone else what you admit now. Why not tell me the truth – this once? It will be a relief to you, psychologically. In the years to come, in prison or out of it, this secret will grow heavy in your mind. You'll long for another opportunity to speak frankly but you won't have it.'

Slowly, Vining shook his head. 'You don't believe me.' He stated it flatly as a fact, his fair face radiant in the lamplight. 'Neither you nor I nor anyone else will ever know the whole truth about this. Or anything else. It's all mystery. One more little puzzle can't add or detract much.' He looked out at the stars and smiled secretly. 'God knows what's up there anyway!'